To: my beautiful granddaughter Jaina R. Abuelita's favorite wrestling Champion 🌟 my Sunshine!! So proud of you 💕 Love you to the moon and back to infinity and beyond forever and ever!!! 🫶 God Bless You! Abuelita Irma

Also by T. Glen Coughlin

ONE SHOT AWAY, A Wrestling Story

Steady Eddie

The Hero of New York

I LOST TO A GIRL
A WRESTLING STORY

T. Glen Coughlin

Copyright 2020 by T. Glen Coughlin

All right reserved.

This is a work of fiction. Names, characters, businesses, places, events and incidents are either the products of the author's imagination or used in a fictitious manner. Any resemblance to actual persons, living or dead, or actual events is purely coincidental.

Published by Under the Flagpole Inc.

Englishtown, NJ

ISBN: 9798699205486

For the one courageous girl who changes everyone's mind.

Chapter 1

COACH RANKIN STEERS me to the center of the wrestling mat and shouts across the gym, "Minutemen, bring it in and take a knee."

Wrestlers, maybe forty in all, tangled in the middle of their moves, turn their heads to look at me, the new kid. I've never changed schools before and the last thing I want is to be put on display to the entire team, but didn't I know this was coming? I shove my hands in the pockets of my ratty Levis and feel their eyes like heat.

"I said, 'Bring it in,'" bellows the coach.

Oversized heavyweights, short and tall middle weights, 100-pound lightweights, flush faced, hair plastered to their heads, t-shirts dark with sweat, make their way across the mat, rip off their headgear, bite into their rubber mouth guards and drop to a knee. "We have a new wrestler," announces the coach. "Mike Brooks. He's a junior and will be coming onto our varsity squad."

"You mean, he's going to try," someone pipes.

A chorus of laughter and slapping five.

I can feel my face reddening by degrees.

The coach folds his arms and waits.

I scan the sweaty faces and settle my gaze on a girl. The only girl. She removes a hair cap and shakes out her mane of chocolate-milk hair. Her wide set green eyes shine in her brown face and look worried.

The coach continues, "Mike moved from Florida to New Jersey. I know a few of you guys might have heard he was coming, might have looked into his win-loss record and what he's achieved. Know this, I don't care about any of that. Today is his first day on our team. He's going to put in the same work as everyone else and have the same opportunities."

Eyes still on me, the girl rises and folds her arms. Her body is tight with muscle, her shoulders wide.

"So join me in welcoming Mike to our team." The coach starts clapping.

For a moment, nothing.

Nada.

Silence.

The team swaps puzzled looks. The coach keeps clapping and shouts, "Come on, I want a warm welcome."

Slowly, wrestlers join in. Beads of sweat roll down my spine. The applause builds. I can't help smiling, at least until I remember my teeth. My crooked teeth.

The clapping dies, all except for one wrestler.

"Alright, that's enough, Mr. Goochinov," says the coach.

At the back of the scrum of wrestlers, one guy has not taken a knee. He continues a slow deliberate clap. An easy five-foot ten, he is slim hipped and lanky with penetrating dark eyes. He wears shorts and a t-shirt that says, "WHATEVER IT TAKES." His jet-black hair is buzzed. His nose is straight and thin, his cheeks hollow.

"Gooch, knock it off!" snaps the coach.

Defiant smile aimed right at me, he brings his hands together one last time and holds them.

The coach leads me into his office and closes the door. I perch on the edge of a bucket chair. The cement block walls are wrapped in wrestling posters.

Champions are MADE here!

Hard work beats talent,
When talent fails,
Work hard.

Things to do today:
   1.   Get up.
   2.   Wrestle.
   3.   Go to bed.

I scan a list of names and weight classes on a white board behind the coach's gunmetal desk. My eyes halt on the girl's name.

Shelby Hoffman – 138 lbs.

She didn't look 138 pounds.

The coach opens a laptop, types, nods at the monitor, then snaps it closed. Under the bright office lights, he looks too old to be a wrestling coach. Hairs snake from his nostrils into his white mustache. His eyebrows are out of control.

He says, "Very impressive stats. Second in the Florida State Tournament two years in a row. How did that feel?"

I don't want to be a wise ass, but ask, "How did what feel?"

"Winning, how did winning feel?"

I tell him second place isn't exactly winning.

"Eighty-six high school wins with two losses in the Florida State's, I'd call that winning."

"I wanted first."

The coach leans back and hooks his hands behind his neck. His stomach swells and strains the buttons on his powder-blue shirt. "We're a small school in a tough wrestling district. Molly Pitcher hasn't produced a state wrestling champ in eighteen years."

I can't think of what to say to that. I've heard the competition in New Jersey is fierce. Worse than Florida.

"Let me tell you a little about me, and then I want to hear about you," says the coach. "I've been around a long time. I've coached just about every sport and learned a few things about winning and losing. Bowling, badminton, wrestling, football, doesn't matter, everybody likes to win. Don't get me wrong, I don't like losing."

I tell him, "Not many people do."

"Here's the most important lesson I've learned." He comes forward and intertwines his fingers. "Sports are not all about winning. It's the journey that's important. I've found that the person you are on the field or on the wrestling mat today, is the person you will be for the rest of your life. So my point is, win or lose, I'm hoping you bring something to the team, some piece that's missing and take something from it that you'll hold onto for your entire life."

I smile and have to say it. "You mean like winning?"

He doesn't laugh. "Let's talk about you. How was your move here?"

I begin with my ride north. My neighbors were traveling to New Jersey to visit their daughter and drove straight through trying to break their best time. "We made it from Daytona to New Jersey in nineteen hours," I say. I don't tell the coach about them refusing to stop when I wanted to go to the bathroom or about the backseat jammed with suitcases and my neighbor's wife telling me to "fit yourself in." I also don't mention the lump of fear jammed in the bottom of my throat that made it hard to swallow.

The coach asks, "And your mother, is she moving here?"

I picture her at the car making a big deal of our last hug; acting like moving away was my idea when I really had no choice. "No, at least not for a while. I'm crashing at my aunt's house."

"Your aunt lives in Molly Pitcher? What's her name? I might know her."

"Maggie."

The coach clicks a ballpoint. "What's her last name?"

I smile because I feel like an idiot. How do I explain that I hardly know my aunt, only met her three times before moving into her house? "She's my real aunt," I say, carefully. "You know like my mother's sister, but I've only called her Aunt Maggie."

"You don't know her last name?"

I sit there like dumb and dumber.

"Well, here's your first wrestling assignment, find out her last name." He laughs and gives me a look that says, I'm hopeless. "Do you know her phone number?"

I tug my phone from my pocket and read the number.

"Tell her I'm going to call her. You do know my name?"

I nod.

"What is it?"

He's making me say it? "Coach Rankin."

"Okay, good. Now some ground rules," says the coach. "We warm up at three, Monday to Friday. Practice at three thirty. If you're late, you'll owe me laps. If you're repeatedly late, don't bother coming. I don't tolerate two things, lateness and apathy."

I'm late for a lot of things, classes, curfews, even dinner, but I'm not late for wrestling practice.

I stand.

He holds me with his eyes and asks, "You do know what apathy means?"

Ah, duh, yes. I glance over my shoulder through the window facing the gym, hoping someone will save me. Half under my breath, I say, "Slackers die many times before their death." It's something I read on a shirt.

"What was that?"

"Apathy means you don't care," I say.

The coach studies me for a few seconds. "Oh, one other thing, your weight. What is it?"

"Right now?"

"Yes, right now." He laughs.

"I cut three to 138."

"You'll have to wrestle-off our current 138," says the coach. "I don't think you'll have a problem."

"You mean the girl?" I picture her lion's mane of hair.

"Our regular wrestler at 138 tore his rotator cuff. So Shelby is just filling an empty slot," he says. "Molly Pitcher doesn't have a girl's team. If we did, she'd be a standout. She puts in the work, but let's face it, boys are boys and girls are girls."

Oh, really, girls are girls, I think. I'll have to write that down.

"Look, don't worry," he says. "Everyone on the team knows the best wrestlers wrestle. That's the rule around here."

I push out of the office door into the gym and walk the edge of the wrestling mats. The air swims with body heat. Guys are executing takedown drills at Goochinov's whistle.

"Time," yells Goochinov.

The wrestlers break apart.

"Face off," shouts Goochinov.

I sit on the bleachers and watch Shelby Hoffman set up for a takedown. She's wearing a red singlet and gym shorts. She glances my way and I suddenly realize she's in my *Writing for College* class. The girl who sits near the window. She drives forward for a double-leg takedown. Her partner throws his legs back in a sprawl and crashes his chest onto her back, trapping her under him.

"Hey Florida," says Goochinov, jogging over. "I heard you're going 138."

I look at him remembering his slow clap.

"I don't know if Rankin told you but the roster is set for the season," he says. "Or was set, until you showed up."

Over Goochinov's shoulder, Shelby gets lifted by her partner and deposited on her butt. Slowly, she gets to her feet and takes her stance.

Not liking his tone of voice I ask, "What's that supposed to mean?"

"If you take Shelby's spot she's off the roster."

"I know, isn't that the way it's supposed to work?"

"You *do* you know who her father is?"

I give a sarcastic, "Mr. Hoffman."

"Exactly right, like in Bruce Hoffman," he says. "The principal and a former running back of the St. Louis Rams."

"The principal here?" I ask. "At Molly Pitcher?"

He nods.

"What are you trying to tell me, that I shouldn't wrestle off his daughter?" I say.

"Exactly, so if I was you, I'd wait this season out." He pats my back.

I laugh and wonder if he's serious. I would never skip a season.

"Alright if we call you Florida? That okay with you, Florida?"

I stare at him and think, give me a break? Florida. It's lame.

"What's the matter, you don't like your new nickname?"

"Gooch!" Coach Rankin's voice echoes through the gym. "Get back on the mat!"

Chapter 2

THE LATE BUS IDLES in the school's parking lot pumping exhaust into the chilly fall air. I cut through the scattered faculty cars. In the distance, the high school's band marches down the football field. The *ump ump* of the tuba carries on the wind.

"Hey, Florida, want a ride?"

It's Goochinov and some of the wrestlers. He's calling from a mustard yellow Mustang. I know enough about cars to know it's a '69 Fastback. A top dollar, collector's car. I jog over.

Goochinov waves his arm out the driver's window and shouts, "No one walks in Jersey. Get in."

I jog around the car to the passenger side and reach for the door handle. He gooses the gas, pulling away. "Come on, run for it," he yells.

I take a step.

He pulls forward, tires chirping, loose asphalt spraying three feet.

I flip them the bird and jam my AirPods in. Tightness travels across my shoulders and into my neck. My fists are balled. In Daytona, my friends said I punched like Mike Tyson and started calling me, Iron Mike. For a while I thought it was cool, but it got around fast and with the nickname came more trouble. I'm in Jersey to avoid trouble and Goochinov is already a pain in my butt hole. A chill travels through my entire body. "You don't want to fight anyone ever again," I whisper.

The song changes to U2's, *With or Without You*. My mother was always playing it when I was kid, always putting her hand under my chin, looking into my eyes and singing, *I can't live with or without you*. I don't know if it was a good thing to sing to a kid or a terrible thing. I set off with an easy jog, trying only to hear Bono's voice in my head. It's two miles and I don't mind the extra work.

Coming down the sidewalk, my aunt's house appears through a row of trimmed hedges. The white-shingled ranch fronts a small porch that barely fits two wooden rockers. It's a very pretty house. Fall flowers that don't grow in Florida line the front garden. The windows are bright and clean. I climb the steps and open an aluminum storm door. The inner door is locked. I consider knocking, then remember my key.

Aunt Maggie calls, "Is that you?"

The house is warm. Something is cooking, something I've never smelled before. Not completely awful, but not good. I follow a dark hall to the kitchen.

She wears her workout clothes from the gym, tights and a t-shirt. The muscles in her arms and legs are firm and defined. It's hard to believe that she's my mother's older sister. Two years apart and she looks so much younger. I suppose all my aunt's aerobics' training keeps her young. My mom thinks spreading a towel and catching rays is a work out.

Aunt Maggie stirs a wooden spoon in a frying pan on the stove and talks on her phone. She tells someone she has to go and turns to me.

"Do you like portabellas?" she asks. "I make sandwiches out of them."

I don't say anything for a moment, just stand there peering at the dark dead-looking disks in the pan. I'm hungry, very hungry. "Is it meat?"

Her laugh comes in a burst. She has a great laugh that you don't expect. "You've never had a portabella?"

"Not that I know of."

"Just like your father," she says. "He'd turn down a gourmet meal for hot dogs and beans." She smiles, sort of cute in an older-lady way.

I drop my backpack on a kitchen chair. I only know certain facts about my father. He was born in Miami, grew up blocks from Daytona Beach and joined the Marines at eighteen. Like me, he never knew his father. I do know my grandmother doesn't like my mother. The last time I purportedly saw her was at my father's funeral. I'd been three years old.

I ask, "Do you think I look like him?"

"Oh, absolutely, yes. I have a few pictures somewhere." She opens a cabinet and pulls out an envelope stuffed with photos. "He was already in the Marines when he started dating your mother. Always coming home, then leaving to some far-off place. When I visited them in Daytona, we all went out a few times, the beach, dinner. It was a long time ago." She gives the pictures a quick look. "These aren't them. But, I'll look later."

I hang there wanting more.

My aunt goes back to the stove.

I wonder what I'm going to eat. I don't have much money and have to keep my calories and carbs down, so places like Micky D's and Burger King don't cut it.

"One more thing," she says. "I wasn't going to bring this up so soon, but I believe in releasing. When I opened the refrigerator this morning to make my a smoothie, guess what?" She moves closer to me, blue eyes blazing, and asks, "What goes in an almond milk smoothie?"

I shrug and remember pouring the end of the container in my cereal.

"Almond milk," she says. "I'm allergic to dairy. So for the time being, could you stick to the skim milk? I'm on a budget and trying to figure out how to afford you." She nudges my shoulder. "Okay?"

Wondering why I'm in New Jersey, why my mother couldn't have chosen me over her boyfriend, Jerry, I agree.

She nods stiffly. "Good, then we'll get along fine."

I shut my door and stomp across my mother's old bedroom. It's a "girly" pink room with white furniture and a frilly bedspread. "Almond milk," I say under my breath. I didn't even know it was almond milk until after I poured it.

I'm thinking this can't be happening to me. I stare at the Joshua Tree poster, probably taped over the bed twenty years ago, and tear it off the wall. I crumple it into a ball and kick it under the bed. The old tape has taken the paint with it. Shit.

I unload my backpack and dig through t-shirts, socks, shorts, jeans and underwear. My money is in a zip-lock bag with my wrestling medals. I dump the bag and count out forty-three dollars. Twenty from my aunt, the rest my "traveling money." Not enough for a plane ticket back to Daytona, that's for sure.

I once asked my mother why she left home. Why didn't she stay in New Jersey?

"Because your grandmother was driving me nuts," she said.

"Why Florida? Why not New York City or Los Angeles?"

"I dropped out of high school and got on a bus. It went one way or the other. I went the other. When I couldn't go any further, I was in Florida."

I pound the window open. The moon hangs like a bright round bulb in the dark sky. Leaves twirl from the trees and pile against a cyclone fence between the houses. It would be a perfect night if it weren't so damn cold. The window slams shut by itself and sounds like a bomb went off.

"What are you doing in there?" calls Aunt Maggie.

"Nothing."

I pull my phone from my pocket and swipe to a photo of Tara on Daytona Beach in a white bikini. We'd just started getting close. Maybe she would have been my first real girlfriend.

I send her a text: *this place sucks – all of it sucks*

Seconds later:

Tara – *are you ok????*

- yea*h but my ants like ths crz lady dont wnt me to drink her almond milk n thres nuting to eat cept fruit n nuts*

Tara - *call your mother and tell her*

- *wht r u doin?*

Tara - *movies*

- *w who*

Tara - *a friend*

- *who??*

Tara - *Tye Dye Luke*

My fingers freeze on the keys. Tie-Dye Luke? The surfer. Drives a Porsche. The only guy in the eleventh grade who calls teachers by their first names and gets away with it.

Tara - *don't be mad*

- *i dont care*

Tara - *don't lie you're jealous*

- *I'm not - hav fun at the movies*

I drop onto the bed. She didn't waste any time. But, why should she? I'm stuck here until I finish high school. I don't like to think past that. It scares me. Without a wrestling scholarship, I'm not going anywhere, except back to Daytona. And then what? Sell Italian ices at the beach? Clean swimming pools?

I find the Minutemen team roster that the coach gave me and save Shelby Hoffman's name and telephone number in my phone. Then, I spend the next twenty minutes entering the rest of the team. Goochinov's words go through my head, *wait this season out.*

If he thinks I'm letting a girl take my spot on the team, he's three fries short of a happy meal, as my old coach used to say.

I check Instagram and skim FB. My home page is lots of

wrestling sites and ridiculous junk; a girl falling in a pool at a twirking contest, a guy kissing a llama on the lips, a dog sleeping with a duck. I search, *Shelby Hoffman NJ*. One hit pops.

I skim her photos - her and friends at the mall, at football games, at the beach emerging from the ocean in bikinis. She's hot, muscular, wrestling hot (if there is such a thing). I look for her father, the principal. No trace of him. She does have a little brother, sort of looks like her. I flip through a few of her wrestling photos, slide the cursor onto the *Friend* button and hit it.

Chapter 3

AROUND AND AROUND the gym we run, under the basketball nets, past the locker room doors, the water fountains, down the other side. One lap – one eighth of a mile. Not wanting to showboat, I stay in the middle of the pack. Above the bleachers, high on the wall, I read the names of the Molly Pitcher State Champions, listed in block letters, one under the other. The last name was added a long time ago. I imagine my name up there, *Michael Brooks – wt. class 138.*

Coach Rankin watches the procession of wrestlers stomp by. "Show me some life out there," he shouts. "My grandmother wears combat boots and runs faster than that."

I catch up to Shelby. "Hey."

She peeks from a hooded sweatshirt. "Coach yells that at every practice."

"How many laps do we have to run?"

"Too many," she says.

"You see that man over there?" She looks to the far end of the gym.

A tall man in a suit and tie watches the wrestlers clop by.

"That's Gooch's father. He donated our uniforms."

I do a double take. "That's pretty generous. What does he do?"

"Exactly do," puffs Shelby. "I don't know, something with investments. I do know he's on Gooch's case twenty-four seven."

I look for Gooch. He's in front of the pack, setting the pace.

"Every summer, Gooch goes to this wrestling camp in Minnesota with the best wrestlers from all over the country," says Shelby. "He hates it."

"I'll go for him," I say.

"I know," she agrees. "My parents wouldn't send me. They tried to talk me into this girls' volleyball camp." She laughs. "I told them I'm a wrestler, not a volleyball player."

Still side-by-side, we turn the corner of the gym and pass under two rows of pull-up bars. "Once, in like the seventh grade, Gooch was pinned in seventeen seconds," she puffs. "His father made him wear a shirt to school that said, *I WILL TRY HARDER* in capital letters."

We jog past Mr. Goochinov. A gold handkerchief in his breast pocket matches his tie. He looks directly at me.

"What's he doing here?" I ask.

"Probably checking you out."

"Me?"

"Yeah. You're big news, especially to me."

I feel my face heat with blood. Shelby steps it up. I stay right with her. I want to ask her what people are saying, but would rather have her come out with it.

Around and around we go. Guys dog it and lag behind. Still, Gooch stays out front.

Rosy cheeked, sweat dripping from her nose, she bumps my

shoulder. "So you're going 138?"

"Yup."

I'm waiting for another question. It doesn't come.

Five minutes later, the coach's whistle sounds. Guys collapse dramatically and lie panting on the mat. The coach walks through them. "Looks like Custer's last stand in here," he says.

Someone grunts, "Custer's last custard."

Someone else, "And I'm whipped cream."

"Who's whipped?" shouts Rankin

The guys let out a collective groan.

"Do you know how far you jogged?" asks Rankin.

Someone shouts, "Ten miles?"

"Three," says Rankin.

"But, it's a sauna in here."

"And it will be hot in here on Saturday when we wrestle the Mustangs," says Rankin. "Now get some water and snap out of your funk."

At the water fountain, Mr. Goochinov closes the space between us and comes along side me. "So you moved here from Florida?" he asks.

I swig water, swallow and wipe my mouth on my sleeve. "From Daytona."

"Permanently?"

"Like until graduation."

"Why now?" he asks.

I glance toward the mats. "I gotta get back."

"Why move here now in the middle of high school?"

I feel a jolt of panic. Do I tell him? Does he already know? I jog away and release a breath I didn't know I was holding.

The team takes a knee around Coach Rankin. "Okay, who can come up here and talk their way through a double-leg?" he asks.

No one moves. Eyes drop to the mat. Shelby either tightens the laces of her wrestling shoes or pretends to.

Seconds pass.

"Lets get the captain up here," says the coach.

Gooch smiles, steps from the pack to the front of the semi-circle and wipes his hands on his baggy basketball shorts.

"And, LaRocca, you just volunteered to be the dummy," says Rankin.

Heads turn to a naturally big kid, who has to weigh at least 195 pounds. He's got blue streaks in his long black hair and a tattoo of a dagger on his shoulder. He yawns and gets to his feet as slow as an old man. After adjusting his kneepads, he steps forward.

"Are we keeping you up?" asks Rankin.

"The Walking Dead had a marathon last night," says LaRocca grinning. He takes a halfhearted stance in front of Gooch.

Rankin sounds his whistle.

Gooch shoots forward. LaRocca sprawls, lands hard on Gooch's back, trapping him. It's a perfect botched double-leg. Gooch lets out a loud groan.

The team cracks up laughing.

Rankin's whistle sounds.

"You almost broke my neck," complains Gooch.

Smirking, LaRocca returns to his place at the back of the pack.

Rankin's whistle drops from his lips. "Let's get two more volunteers up here."

Again, no one moves.

"Mike, why don't you come on up," says the coach.

My plan was to operate in stealth mode and lie low. Everyone turns to me.

The coach claps his hands. "Dustin, come on up. You be the dummy for Mike."

Dustin looks like he'd been asked to sniff a dog's butt. He stands across from me, hands on his hips. I picture the chart from Rankin's office. Dustin is the 160-pounder. Short and dense with muscle.

"Florida show us how you learned it way down south," someone shouts.

The team cracks up.

I assume a staggered leg stance. Dustin crouches in front of me. I lead with my left hand, grab Dustin's arm. Right hand protecting my legs, I step in and apply pressure to the back of Dustin's head. Like most wrestlers, he pushes against my hand. I release, step in low, grab his knees and dump him on his butt.

I hop to my feet and extend my hand to Dustin. He takes it and I pull him up.

"I like it," says Coach Rankin. "Nice, very nice. What is your favorite move? Your go-to move?"

I don't want to be doing this. "Fireman's carry."

"Walk the team through it," says Rankin.

Some of the guys moan.

"Come on," says Rankin. "Let's break it down at half speed."

I square my shoulders in front of Dustin. The arm grip is the key. I always hit the move from an inside bicep tie on the arm. I drop to my knees, tuck my head under Dustin's arm, drape him over me, lower my body and dump him over my shoulder onto his back.

"I think we can put this in our drills," says Rankin.

The rest of the practice feels good. Paired with Gooch, I am quickly drenched in sweat. My old rhythms and mechanics switch to autopilot - grip, pull, tug and tumble.

"Here's the thing about our team," says Gooch as we tie up. "We lost two good guys when Rankin took over as the coach."

I slip my arm over his shoulder.

"This is Rankin's first season as head coach," he says. "He used to be the assistant coach. Now it's only him. I got voted team captain. So I sort of took things over. Rankin lets me run most of the practices."

Surprised to hear this, I glance over at the coach. He's walking through the wrestlers with a whistle in his lips.

Gooch continues, "And you can see how old he is. I heard Principal Hoffman tried to force him into retirement. Rankin threatened to sue the school district for age discrimination. So we're stuck with him."

Gooch talking about the coach, when the guy is obviously trying his best, pisses me off. I snap Gooch's head down and take a clean fast shot. I lift and dump him high and hard to the mat. He tumbles back and gives me a surprised look. "Dude, this is practice," he croaks. "Take it easy."

The gym door opens. A well-built man in a blue suit, handsome, but somehow scary with serious gray eyes and dark skin, enters and sits in the bleachers.

"Is that Shelby's father?" I ask.

Gooch smiles. "Yeah and he's not going to like you much when you take his daughter's starting position away."

My eyes find Shelby, then shoot back to her father. I think about pinning her, a girl, and taking her weight class. I know she's no match for me and yet, I have an anxious feeling in my gut. I've never felt this way about winning and wish it would stop.

Chapter 4

THURSDAY, AFTER PRACTICE, it rains. I board the late bus and slide into the last bench with my wrestling bag on my lap. I'm so hungry, my stomach hurts. I bought an apple and a cheese stick at lunch to keep my calories in check. In Daytona, staying on my diet was easier. Kids ate off-campus at a row of restaurants that catered to the teachers and students. When I had money, I chowed down on healthy foods like grilled fish over vegetables. No one is allowed to leave the grounds at Molly Pitcher High. Even if they did, without a car there's nowhere to go.

Long distance runners, willowy as onion grass file down the main row. They crash weighty backpacks onto the seats. Some of the girls wear shorts and pull their long legs to their chests. A pretty girl with shiny hair smiles at me. I smile back, remember my teeth and try a grin.

"What sport?" she asks.

I remove my AirPods. "Wrestling."

She thinks about this. "I thought so. You look like a wrestler. You new here?"

"Yup, from Daytona."

"I heard of the Daytona 500."

"I lived about two miles from the race track." I wait for another question, hope for one. The girls share a whisper and laugh.

I tap one girl on the shoulder. "What does a wrestler look like?"

The girls blink, turn to each other, then back at me. One says, "They kinda walk hunched over and stiff like their bodies hurt." Then, they both giggle. "And they have those big necks with the muscles popping on the sides."

I laugh.

"And what about the celery sticks," the other girl says. "I mean, is that all you guys eat?"

"Sometimes carrots," I say.

Giggling, the girls turn around.

I'm left looking at the back of their heads. I listen to the soft splatter of rain on the roof of the bus and insert my AirPods. Bono is singing the live version of *Where the Streets Have No Name*, which is sort of the way I feel.

"Yo, Florida," yells Dustin. "You too good to sit with us?"

Grabbing the seat backs, I move to a bench across from him. "You *are* going to wrestle Shelby off?" he asks loudly so the others can hear.

"Who are you?" I say. "Captain Obvious?"

A few guys laugh.

"I saw her weigh in this morning after gym class. One thirty on the dot," says Dustin.

"Was she naked?" someone smirks.

"Yeah in your dreams," says Dustin.

"Florida, you're doing us a favor," says LaRocca. "She kills our lineup, loses every week. She's the only girl in the entire school forcing her way onto our team. I don't even like to touch her. It's totally weird. We're the Minutemen, right? Not the Minutegirls."

Guys crack up laughing, like what LaRocca said was hilarious.

"What's with Goochinov?" I ask. "How come he wants her on the team so bad?"

Everyone's eyes light for a second. They exchange glances.

"That's the never ending saga," says LaRocca. "Gooch wrestled her off and took her weight class at 132, bumping her to 138. He tries to pretend that she's just another dude on the team who happens to have nice boobs and junk in the trunk, but he can't because they've been going out, off and on, since the seventh grade."

"Or, maybe, Shelby lost her wrestle off on purpose so Gooch could stay at 132," says Dustin. "She went to 138 and now they both get to wrestle and get their varsity letters."

"Maybe Shelby lost something else too," smirks LaRocca. "Something you can't get back, and now Gooch thinks he owes her."

I sort of cringe, because that's a shitty thing to say. No one is laughing.

LaRocca lowers his ball cap over his eyes and folds his arms like he's going to take a nap. "So, here's the bottom line," he says with a yawn. "Florida, when you walked on to the team, you did us all a favor."

I think about Shelby throwing her wrestle-off with Gooch. It doesn't seem possible. Even if she does earn a varsity letter, would she settle for wrestling up a weight class and a losing season?

Strip malls, pizza joints, gas stations and supermarkets flash by. Gooch zooms past the bus in his yellow Mustang. For the briefest moment, I glimpse Shelby in the passenger seat. The bus brakes and squeaks to a stop. The bus starts again, hits a bump. Everyone bounces into the air. Some of the girls shout, "Whoa!"

"That's Mount Rushover," says LaRocca. "Everyday we crack our skulls on the top of this old bus. It's about as much fun you're ever going to have in Molly Pitcher." He smiles, then shouts, "NOT!"

I find aunt Maggie reclined in her lounge chair. She clicks off the TV. "Good, you're home," she says. "We need to talk."

I follow her into the kitchen where there's nothing cooking on the stove. No food in sight.

"I arranged something for you," she says. "Sort of a surprise depending how you look at it." She turns on the faucet and rinses a coffee cup. "I would imagine you'll go to the mall on the weekends with the friends you are going to make, right?"

Not liking the question, I shrug.

"Drink those fancy lattes and cappuccinos at Starbucks?"

"Not during the season," I say.

She smiles and taps her finger on my chest. "Well, one way or the other, you will need spending money, true or false?"

"I guess."

"No, not 'I guess,'" she says. "True or false."

"Yes, true."

"Good," she says. "Because then you'll like the surprise. Molly Pitcher is an expensive place to live." She opens the refrigerator. "Did you eat dinner?"

"No."

"You must be hungry." She lets out a laugh. "If I remember right, teenage boys are always hungry."

Besides her vitamins, yogurts, fruit and condiments, the frig is empty.

"I'm sorry but I didn't have time to shop," she says and hands me a yogurt. She digs into the pantry and comes out with a box of protein bars.

"These are meal replacements," she says reading the back of the box. "Two hundred and fifty calories, one gram of fat, twenty grams of protein." She tears the box open. "You need protein to maintain all that muscle you're carrying."

I take a bar and feel its weight. It's practically nothing.

"Don't look at me like that," she says, "I eat those things all the time. Put a few in your pocket, because we've got to get going. Later, we'll stop at the grocery store."

"Get going where?"

"That's part of the surprise."

"I don't like surprises," I say, unable to remove the edge from my voice.

"Did you shower?" she asks.

"At school."

"Good, put on some slacks and a clean shirt."

With my back on my bedroom door, I slide to the floor feeling crumpled and small. "Slacks?" I say out loud. "What are slacks?"

I open my laptop. On FB, I see:

Mike Brooks and Shelby Hoffman are now friends.

My eyes stop on the news feed.

Zach Goochinov posted a photo of me in the school parking lot flipping the bird. The caption is:

- wut up w FL Mike acting all thirsty

Comments trail down the page:

- you see his teeth

- I think he otta google hick n update his profile pic

- LMAO

- you see his sneaks!!!

- flea market find.

Shelby Hoffman: *get over your selves*

Adam LaRocca: *O like he never heard of NIKE???*

- like they don't have dentists in FL

Zach Goochinov: *i don't think they do...LOL*

- like they don't sell brand name in FL

- like he woke and is our fam?? NOT!

Zach Goochinov: *I look at Fl Mike and get the hick-ups LOL*

- If I had teeth like his id put dentures in my a-hole n walk backwards

9 people like this post

Comments are popping onto the screen one after the other. I can't take my eyes off them. They are talking about me.

Me!

In Daytona I hadn't been exactly Joe Popular but I had friends. Real friends.

I slam the laptop closed. I want to throw it through the window. Inside, I ache. How could these be the same guys I'd just wrestled with? The guys I'm supposed to call teammates?

I find a hand mirror on the cluttered vanity and sweep my hair from my forehead. I dig my nails into a patch of zits and wipe the puss away with a tissue. Tears burn in my eyes. How is Shelby or any girl ever going to like a guy with bad teeth and zits? I try a smile. It's like God gave me too many teeth, like they all sprouted into the same too-crowded space. A tear drips down my cheek.

I call my mother, listen to a far-away ring and imagine her phone on the kitchen table, buzzing in a half circle like a dying palmetto bug.

"Hey, what's up?" says Jerry.

"My mom. Can I talk to her?"

"Remember what you did to my bike?" he asks.

I was mowing the lawn. I asked him to move his motorcycle off the grass. He didn't move it, just worked the last puff of smoke from his cigarette and blew it in my face. When I knocked the kickstand in, the bike tipped and snapped the clutch pedal.

"You don't remember?" he asks.

I picture Jerry holding the phone, eyes creased, toothpick rolling between his lips, enjoying every moment he gets to torture me. "You don't let me forget."

"Then you still owe me sixty bucks for a new clutch pedal."

"Jerry, is my mom there?"

"How do you plan on paying me back? How about getting that aunt of yours to write a check?"

"Is my mom there or not?"

"She might be. Do you want to talk to her?"

"Yes."

"Yes what?"

"Jerry, come on, stop breaking balls."

"Yes, what?"

"Please can I speak to her?"

"That's better, but it's not a good time. She's in the middle of something very important."

In the background, I hear my mother say, "Jerry, give me the damn phone, now."

The phone clatters. "Honey?"

"Mom."

"Are you okay?"

My voice disintegrates to a whine, "I need to come home. Things here aren't good."

"Now come on, you just got there."

"Aunt Maggie is a little crazy."

"Your aunt is actually very smart. I'll admit, a bit eccentric."

"A bit?"

"You need to get to know her. Give her a chance. She never had kids and she's been living alone for a long time. Be patient."

"Do you know what she made for dinner tonight?" I whisper. "Nothing. She gave me a box of protein bars, like I'm supposed to eat ten of them."

"I'm sure-."

"No Mom," I cut in. "She doesn't want me here. She doesn't even want me drinking her almond milk. Your room, it smells old, like stale clothes. It's the same way you left it. She really doesn't want me here, and you had to beg her to take me, didn't you?"

Silence. My mother won't talk honestly with Jerry listening.

Even to this day, I can't figure out how Jerry wormed his way into our house. About two years ago, he slept over and appeared at breakfast in his white carpenter jeans, boots and leather vest, arms sleeved in smeary tats, dirty blonde hair pulled in a pony. "Little man," he announced. "You're mother over there is cooking me some eggs. Why don't you pull up a chair?"

Through the phone, I hear a door shut.

"Listen to me," she whispers. "You can't come home right now and you know that. Jerry is getting me back on my feet. He paid some of the back taxes on the house."

Getting *you* back on your feet? Getting *you* and not *us*?

"I can't have things go," she hesitates, "go back to the way they were. And don't put this on me. You did this, not me."

I ask, "Is he listening right now?"

"No, I'm in the bathroom. I locked the door." I hear the water running in the sink.

"Mom, please. I'll get a job. You know I'm a hard worker."

"Give your aunt a chance. Do it for me."

I tell her about the wrestling team, about having to wrestle-off the principal's daughter. My mother doesn't say anything. I wonder if she's even listening.

"Did you hear me?" I say louder. "The principal's daughter! I'm the walk-on. The spoiler. When I beat her she'll be bounced to JV. She won't earn a varsity letter."

My mom sort of laughs, "Maybe she'll surprise you."

"What?"

"Maybe you'll be on JV."

I wait for her to say more and feel trapped. "You really think I'd let that happen?"

"Why, because she's a girl?"

"No, Ma, because I'm not about losing and you know that."

"Honey, Jerry's is going to break the door down if I don't open it," she says. "We'll talk tomorrow. Love you. Be nice to my sister."

Chapter 5

WE DRIVE TO MY AUNT'S GYM, which is this ginormous place, about the size of a COSTCO. She still won't tell me the surprise. At the front desk, she introduces me to Tony, the manager of *Work-Out-World, More than a Gym, A Way of Life.*

"Come with me," says Tony.

I'm thinking, Oh cool, my aunt signed me up for a gym membership. He leads me into the men's locker room, opens a cabinet and hands me a shirt. "Go ahead," he says, "put it on."

A free shirt! I yank my Daytona Beach High School Wrestling shirt off and pull on a powder-blue polo with the logo, "W-O-W," embroidered on the breast pocket.

"There really isn't much too it," he says. "But, it will keep you busy."

I ask, "Much to what?"

"The job." He digs into the cabinet, moving brooms and mops around.

I swallow and scan a shelf of cleaning supplies, rolls of paper towels and toilet paper.

"You ever work one of these?" He lifts a mop from a sudsy

plastic bucket. "Think, figure eight. Nothing to it."

He leans over his bulging stomach and works the mop across the locker room floor. After two figure eights, he's winded. For a guy who manages a gym, he's in no kind of shape.

"So here's the deal," says Tony. "Take care of this locker room before closing time, Monday to Friday, and you get a free membership and a weekly salary."

I watch him with suspect eyes. For the moment, I've completely suspended all belief that this is happening to me. Could this really be my aunt's surprise? A job cleaning a locker room? A swell of rage moves like a cloud across my chest. I've been at her house less than a week and she's already found me a lousy job, found me a job without asking me if I'm interested in mopping floors.

Tony continues, "As long as the mirrors are wiped, the paper receptacles filled, the floor sparkling, trash emptied, I'm happy." He drops the mop head into the bucket. "You can figure out your own hours. Come two hours before closing, come right after school, work out, then clean this place, it's up to you. And listen, I've had kids doing this job who thought they were better than it. I'm the first to admit it's not glamorous, but it's honest work. Leave this place clean every night and you'll have the satisfaction of a job well done."

My eyes follow a group of guys in workout gear.

"You getting this?" asks Tony.

Still, I say nothing.

Tony takes a long look at me. "Your aunt is good people.

She's been here for ten years. She's like family." His eyes remain fixed on mine. "I'm doing this for her. She asked me. No one is going to break your chops about coming and going. You want to sneak in here and clean when the place is empty, be my guest. Just make sure everything sparkles at closing time. You got that?"

I glare at him and don't drop my eyes. "How much?"

"A hundred a week. Cash."

I do the math in my head. Five days equals twenty a day. What I don't know is how many hours a day I'll be swinging that mop. "Let's make it one-twenty five."

Tony's face sags. "How about a hundred and ten?"

We shake hands and seal the deal.

"Listen, if you need to talk to someone, I'm here," says Tony. "My old man left when I was five, moved out west, never came back. My mother, she, well, let's just say could have done things differently, but now I manage this place. I'm doing okay."

"My father didn't leave me," I say. "He was a Marine, killed in action."

"Yeah, well," says Tony. "Sorry 'bout that. How old were you?"

I don't bother to answer.

"You don't have to talk about it. I understand. That's fine too." He shuts the storage cabinet door and leaves.

I pass the lockers and enter the large bathroom. A sink is coated with whiskers. Shaving cream is smeared on the granite countertop. I consider calling my mother, consider ripping off my "W-O-W" shirt and walking out. Then I think about having a hundred and ten dollars in my pocket.

In my head, my aunt's voice vibrates like too much bass, *you will need spend money, true or false?* I turn on the water and return to the closet for a sponge.

True.

When the locker room is clean, I navigate through the gym in my new club shirt. A large expanse of gray machines and free weights reflect in the mirrored walls. A muscular man in nylon shorts and a sleeveless t-shirt works a forty-pound dumbbell behind his head. Each upward stroke flexes his triceps into hard loaves of bread. Through a floor to ceiling window, I watch my aunt lead women in a fast-paced dance routine. Hips and arms wag and flail to a pounding dance beat.

Every night, I think. Practice ends around five, get to my aunt's house, eat (or not eat), bike here, clean the locker room. I wipe a coating of sweat off the back of my neck.

"No spying on the ladies."

My heart leaps. I turn around quick.

Shelby's eyes wheel from my face to the logo on my shirt. "You work here?"

"My aunt is the aerobics instructor. She got me a job."

"So you work here?" she asks again.

"Yeah."

"Doing what?"

I search for the right word. "I'm an attendant."

"An attendant of what?"

"I keep an eye on things."

Considering this, she twists her mouth to the side and bites her lip. "According to what I'm hearing, you're supposed to be unbeatable."

"I want to be," I say.

She laughs and flicks her hair over her shoulder. "Bring it on, that's all I have to say. I'm not going to get psyched out by everyone on the team talking like you're some kind of messiah here to save them."

"Me?" I say, pulse quickening.

"I don't care how many matches you won in Florida," she says sharply. "You won't embarrass me. I know how to wrestle."

"Hold on," I say. "How much do you weigh?"

"I'm 131."

"How do you expect to win if you're wrestling at 138?"

She looks like she's trying to find the answer. "Well, Gooch is 132," she says. "I wrestled him off and he beat me."

"Beat you how?"

"The usual way," she says.

"Did he pin you?"

"No."

"What about cutting to 126?" I ask.

"Like I haven't thought of that. Jimmy Webster is expected to go to state this year."

"You could try."

"I did try." She takes two steps then turns back. "You've

been in Jersey like five minutes. You don't know anything about the team or me."

I feel myself blushing. "Do you win at 138?"

She frowns. "Not a lot."

"I could teach you some techniques. My old coach wrestled for Germany in the Olympics. He taught me some cool throws."

She places her finger an inch from my nose. Her nail is bitten, pink and sore looking. "Wrestle me off," she says. "Maybe you're the one who has to worry."

"I was just-."

"Well don't. I'm not fragile. I don't require special handling."

She turns and heads away.

I wander back to the locker room and swish the mop across the floor. I read a poster on the wall.

Best things to do today:
1. *Work out*
2. *Have a healthy shake at our snack bar*
3. *Gather with friends and family*
4. *Eat two pieces of fruit*
5. *Watch your carbs*
   From Your Friends at W-O-W.

I grab the glass cleaner and head to the mirrors. Leaning over the counter top, I wipe, stop, stare at myself, and touch the hint of whiskers above my lip and shades of a goatee on my chin. I turn my head one way then the other. I'm not as handsome as Gooch. I've had my nose broken in a match. It healed crooked. And my teeth, well, forget them. Maybe if I cut my hair, I'd at least look like a Jersey guy. I try a smile and hear Jerry's voice in my head. *Damn kid, your mouth looks like the demolition derby.*

Chapter 6

MONDAY, I peddle my aunt's bike to the high school. It's a red rickety old tank with fat fenders and a loose chain guard. With no gears on the bike and the hilly roads, it's a decent work out. I arrive before the buses. The cold Jersey morning turned my hands and feet to ice. Untangling the bike lock from the wire basket over the front fender is torture. A pumpkin orange Dodge Challenger zooms around the parking lot. I glimpse Adam LaRocca's blue hair inside the car.

"Get a horse," someone yells out the window.

Real funny.

The weekend turned out pretty good. After a short Saturday practice, my aunt and I hit the sales at the mall. She let me pick out a pair of Nikes, socks, underwear, t-shirts and jeans, and paid for everything. We chowed down at Ruby Tuesday's, both ordering the grilled sole and the salad bar. She asked a lot of questions about my mother. Was Annie working? Was Annie still smoking? What was her diet like? Did she go to the beach? Did she wear sunscreen? Was she still drinking? Was she happy?

I proceeded with caution. Part of me wondered if my aunt really cared or was she just being nosy. I told her my mother only smoked when she drank. I didn't tell her she drank every day and didn't tell her about the vodka bottle under the sink and didn't mention that she practically survives on cranberry screwdrivers and canned beer nuts.

I get the lock untangled and guide the chain through the front tire. When I look up, Zach Goochinov is crossing a stretch of grass toward the bike rack. He's wearing faded jeans, yellow high-topped vintage Jordan's and a long sleeve t-shirt that says, *Wrestling - It Doesn't Taste Like Chicken*. Like a lot of the Jersey guys, he's coatless and acting like it's warm outside.

He looks over my bike and smiles. "You could be riding a collectable. Run it on EBay, maybe it's worth fifty bucks?" He throws his leg over the frame and bounces up and down on the rubber seat. "It's got a few scratches, but-."

I can feel myself tensing up. "What do you want?"

Gooch places a cigarette in his lips. He lights it and inhales. "Want one?"

I give him a face like you've got to be a complete asshole. "You smoke?"

"I'm quitting," says Gooch. "This might be my last smoke until the end of the season."

He takes another drag.

Plenty of guys at my old high school spent their days bumming cigs and spare change, always posing, always sneaking around like they were escaped juvies. But, not the wrestlers. None of us would ever smoke.

"You're supposed to be the captain," I say. "Put that thing out."

Gooch holds the burning cig next to his thigh and watches the footpath that winds around the school. He's about to take a puff.

"Now," I say.

He flicks the cig in the grass. "You do realize," he says with smoke coming out his nose, "that Rankin holds wrestle-offs on Mondays and today is Monday. He's going to expect you to wrestle-off Shelby. If you do, you'll put her on JV or completely out for the season. You do realize that?"

"That's the way it works," I say. "Right?"

Seconds pass.

"You know, you're funny," he says with an attitude. "Or trying to be funny. I'm not sure."

I get the feeling that he might take a swing at me. He eyes me, like he's sizing me up, judging me. I remove my hands from my pockets. His smile reminds me of a space alien before it eats its victim. "Look, I'm going to say it straight out, don't wrestle her off."

"What?" I say. "No way."

His eyes blink as if he can't believe what he's hearing. "It's about what's right," he says. "You just don't come onto our team and destroy a wrestler who's been working for a varsity letter since the eighth grade."

"Destroy?" I say.

"Yeah, because it would destroy her."

The sun breaks from a cloud. Our shadows appear on the cut wet grass.

"Dude, listen," he says. "There's a lot of shit you don't know about this team and this school. Shelby has no one on her side. You want to hear what Coach Rankin actually said to my father?"

I do want to hear this. "What?"

"My father had Rankin on speaker phone. I was outside his office door and I hear Rankin say Shelby is just filling a slot so the team doesn't have to forfeit. That's cold, isn't it? I mean she broke her butt for three years on JV, finally gets a spot on varsity and she's just filling a slot?"

"It's not cold," I say. "It's wrestling."

"I don't see it that way. All my life coaches told me it's all about the team," he says. "Team, team, team. And then you reach varsity and you find out it's not all about the team. It's only about winning? Nah, I don't accept that."

"Losing sucks," I say. "You learn from it, but it still sucks."

Gooch coughs out a laugh.

"You think that's funny?" I ask.

"No, not what you said. You. You crack me up. You come into my school with your tan and your surfer-dude hair and think you can put Shelby on JV? No questions asked? Why don't you wrestle JV and wait your turn? You're a junior. She's a senior. This is Shelby's last shot for a varsity letter."

I remember a vocabulary word my English teacher liked to use. Malice. Yes, there is malice in Gooch's words and in his fixed smile.

"I heard you're mopping the floors at Work-Out-World and had a chat with Shelby," says Gooch. "What was that all about?"

"It wasn't about anything," I say.

"Dude, you gotta understand," he says. "You make a move in this town, you bump into me. Here's some advice, stay away from her." He grabs my arm at the elbow. "You don't need to be her jogging partner at practice. You don't ever need to be near her. If you have any ideas about her, I'd seriously reconsider."

I pull out of his grasp. "Is she your girlfriend?"

"That's none of your business."

"Didn't you wrestle her off?" I ask, knowing the answer.

"If you could call it that," he says.

"You had no problem bouncing her out of her weight class. Did you?"

"What you don't get is as far as I'm concerned you shouldn't exist. You haven't earned anything at our school. You don't get the right to have an opinion."

"Shelby says you didn't pin her." I watch my words sink in.

Gooch throws his hands up. "I didn't have to pin her and I didn't want to pin her in front of her father. Is that okay with you?"

The last bus in the long line pulls away leaving behind a spew of black diesel. I side step Gooch and walk toward the main doors.

"Hold up," calls Gooch.

I keep walking.

He jogs up. "Dude wait, okay?"

I stop.

"Look, I know you're hard core. You eat, breathe and crap

wrestling. Shelby and me, we're not like that. We're not going to the States. Not even thinking about going. We don't walk the halls spitting into a cup so we can make weight and we're absolutely not wrestling in college. I plan on having a good time, not sweating my balls off in some foam-padded dungeon with a bunch of dudes. But Shelby still needs to be on varsity this year. Her father expects it. She put in the work and she deserves her letter."

"Not after she loses to me," I say.

A bell rings. A teacher begins closing the front doors, giving each a hard clicking pull. The teacher smiles as we enter the school. "Mr. Goochinov," she says. "Glad you could join us today."

All morning I shuffle class-to-class, doodling in my new notebook, thinking about what Gooch said. Part of me wants to starve and wrestle-off him, put him on the JV squad. Give him what he deserves. Why is he wrestling if he's not really into it? If he needs something to list on his college apps, he should join the debate team or the student council. The pushy prick with his toothpaste-commercial smile would be a star in the drama club. And if Shelby wasn't "all about wrestling," why should I care about bouncing her to JV? Isn't that how you tell the champions from the chumps? The chumps act like they care, even put in some work, but if practice is suddenly cancelled, they're the first ones high-fiving and celebrating.

In Marine Biology, a substitute kills the lights. Movie time. The class gives a sigh of relief and takes out their phones. On a wall mounted flat-screen, a bask of crocodiles compete with a pod of hippopotamus in a dwindling African river. A deadly serious narrator announces, "It is a time of drought in the African savanna."

The documentary is brutal. A crocodile spins a baby hippo around in its clamped jaws. A two-ton hippo stomps on a croc. A croc rips the hindquarters off a mama hippo. The class cheers when a hippo chomps its jaws into a croc. The battle takes place in a foot of brown water until the sunbaked animals stand bewildered and withered like mud-caked statues. Many die of starvation. Hyenas and vultures rip and tear at carcasses. Then, mercifully, the rains come. Frogs emerge from the mud banks and the baritone announcer states, "Another rainy season brings new life and struggles to this river where nature rules supreme."

Lunch period. The cavernous cafeteria echoes with laughter and loud conversations. Varsity wrestlers commandeer the table near the doors. LaRocca at one end. Moose, the heavy weight, at the other. Some girls who hang around practice are sprinkled between them. One, an Asian girl with porcelain skin and silk black hair, giggles as I pass carrying an applesauce, a chicken salad and a skim milk. Someone shouts, "I thought Kurt Cobain was dead. Dude cut your hair!"

I don't react or turn around.

I place my tray on an empty table near the windows. Outside, rain pelts cars and runs in rivulets along the curbs. My eyes settle on Gooch's Mustang in the student lot. The foggy passenger window is cracked open. A barely visible trail of smoke leaks into the windy day. Could Shelby be in there with Gooch? He said they were tight.

Eyes on the car, I open my carton of milk, drink half, wolf down my applesauce, then poke my salad. I don't add the dressing.

"So Mister Brooks, how was your first week at Molly Pitcher?" Principal Hoffman in shirt and tie stands framed by the window.

Mouth ajar, I shove my chair out and begin to stand.

"No, no, please, enjoy your lunch," he says. "I'm making my rounds and saw you over here in no-man's land."

Half chewed chicken in my mouth, I swallow and manage a few words.

"Are you settling in?"

"Yes, sir, absolutely." I want to flee. What am I going to say if the Principal asks about the wrestle-off?

"I heard you met my Shelby at her gym and you have a job there. I hope it's not going to be too much for you."

"No, sir. I can wrestle and work."

His smile drops. "You forgot something."

I wait, trying to read his face.

"Your school work?" he says. "It comes first. Knowledge is power, remember that."

"Right," I say.

The principal pulls out a chair and sits. His big knees look hard and round under sharply creased dress slacks.

Heads are turning in the cafeteria. Conversations dying.

"Have you thought about college?" he asks.

"I'd like to get back to Florida. Be near my mother."

"There are plenty of good schools there. You should start narrowing your sights on three or four. I saw your transcript. Your grades should be competitive at some universities."

"You saw my grades?"

"Part of my job is to get you ready for the next step," he says. "As a junior, you'll be taking your S-A-T. Early college applications should be in the mail next fall. With wrestling and first-class grades, you'll be in good shape."

I sneak a look at the wrestler's table. All eyes are on me.

"I'll schedule you an appointment with your guidance counselor." He stands, broad as a billboard.

As the principal walks away, I slide my eyes to Gooch's Mustang. The windows are completely steamed over.

That afternoon the locker room is packed, rowdy and hot. The smell of stale t-shirts, socks and jocks left over night to dry on wire lockers is thick as armpit stank. My locker is at the end of the row, closest to the urinals. I change out of my street clothes and try to ignore a game of "keep away" as someone's shoe sails overhead.

"You going for it?"

It's Mookie, the 106-pounder, wearing a flat brimmed Yankee hat and an oversize T-shirt that says, "Live the Dream."

"Going for what?" I ask.

"For 138."

"Of course."

"Cool," says Mookie, "because she sucks."

"I think she's pretty cool," I say, and leave the locker room. At an open spot on the mat, I begin shoulder stretches, one arm at a time across my chest.

Guys spread out in the bleachers with snacks and sports drinks. Counting the freshman and JV, it's maybe forty wrestlers. Shelby is jumping rope on a patch of hardwood. The rope whistles through the air.

I jog around the gym and stop at the coach's office. "Do you have a minute?" I ask poking my head in the door.

Rankin's eyes lift from his laptop. "No, I'll give you fifty seconds," he says. "We've got a lot to cover today."

"I'm thinking about wrestling off Gooch for 132," I say.

Rankin removes his reading glasses. "You're thinking?"

"Yeah."

"Well, here's my advice, stop thinking. Let me do the thinking. You wrestle. I coach. Okay? How does that sound?"

"The thing is-."

Rankin leans forward. His large head eclipses his desk lamp. "Mike, you're 141-pounds. You could spit off three pounds. Skip breakfast and you make weight. You'll win at 138. Maybe go all the way to the States. I'm not letting you cut to 132. Why do that to yourself?"

I think, because Gooch needs to be demolished.

Rankin waves his hand. "If you wrestled 132, what do I do with Gooch? Where does he fit? He's one of my solid wrestlers." He points to the chart on the white board. "It's the domino effect. Gooch would have to go up to 138. I don't think he can win at that weight." The coach slides closer and almost whispers, "Let Shelby go to field hockey or volleyball with the girls. That's where she belongs. She's a lovely person, a great competitor, but who ever heard of having a girl on a boy's wrestling team in the first place? This Title 9, it's a pain in my you-know-what. But, you can't put the genie back in the bottle, can you? It would be another story if Shelby had the skills to compete on a boy's varsity level, then yes, maybe I'd have to agree. She might belong, but under the circumstances," he sighs. "I know it's rough on her."

I take a breath between my teeth knowing this was a dumb thing to ask the coach. I shouldn't have let Gooch get to me.

Sounding weary, the coach says, "I told you the best wrestler wrestles, that's the bottom line. You owe this to yourself and the team."

I know the coach is right.

"And besides," says Rankin. "I'm trying to coach a wrestling team. Half you guys can't keep your eyes off her. If she were one of the boys, would you be worrying? You've been in town for what, ten days and you're already smitten. Believe me, you're not the first Mister Brooks and you won't be the last. So go warm up. You're wrestling her off."

At the side of the gym, Shelby stretches, legs wide apart, twisting at the waist, touching her fingertips to the toes of her wrestling shoes. Half the guys on the team are checking her out.

Gooch is on the mat talking to LaRocca. They glance at me and resume their conversation.

I should warm up. I don't want to pull a muscle. I'll go easy on her, give her a full minute, then go for a quick pin. I take a deep breath and begin jumping jacks, move to sit-ups and end with pull-ups on the bar.

Rankin strides to the center of the mat and blows his whistle. His words about Shelby loop in my head - *if she were one of the boys - can't keep your eyes off her - to field hockey or volleyball with the girls.* I wonder what would happen if I told Principal Hoffman about the coach's real feelings.

"I want to get the wrestle-offs over," announces Rankin to anyone listening.

Every wrestler in the gym cranes their neck to look at me.

Some one calls out, "I challenge Bill Robinson."

A tall, loose-limbed boy with knobby knees and soft eyes rises from a circle of freshmen. To me, he looks more likely to be zipping a sidewalk on a skateboard rather than challenging a 195-pound varsity wrestler.

Bill Robinson, an oil drum with a head, snorts and stomps his way to the center of the mat. The freshman doesn't look impressed. He bounces on his toes and snaps his chinstrap.

The team spreads out around the circle.

Rankin says a few words to Robinson and the freshman, then backs away and sounds his whistle.

The freshman and Robinson tie up and fight for inside arm position. Robinson looks unmovable, a bulldozer stuck in first gear. He shoves the freshman around the mat.

I catch Shelby's eye.

She looks away.

Chicken churns in my stomach. I make a beeline for the locker room. In the lavatory, I bang open a stall and gag. Nothing comes up.

"Yo, you in here?" Gooch with LaRocca towering behind, block the doorway. They wear sweats and hoodies like two rappers.

"Here's what I was thinking," says Gooch. "You give Shelby the first three matches of the season. Win or lose, she gets the matches on her varsity record and earns her letter." He forces a smile. "It was Shelby's idea."

There's no way I am going for this and I can't picture this proposal coming from Shelby.

"And she told me to tell you no goosing the kadunk-a-dunk," laughs LaRocca.

"So today I'm supposed to do what?" I ask.

"That's the beauty of it," smiles Gooch. "You don't have to do anything. You just tell Rankin you're not wrestling her off."

"I don't think so," I reply.

"Or I could make sure you don't wrestle," says Gooch.

"And how are you going to do that?" I ask.

Like a classic wuss, he doesn't move. I'm hoping he does because I'm so ready. A warm feeling floods my core. It's the same feeling I have when I'm around my mother's boyfriends. Like anything could happen. Anything will happen.

"Hold on," says LaRocca. "Gooch, do we really want her on the team?"

Gooch gives LaRocca a surprised look. "What the hell, I thought we-."

"We could be rid of her," says LaRocca. "I mean aren't you sick of her parading around acting like she's one of us?"

"Us?"

"You know, like a dude."

"No, that's your problem," says Gooch.

I stand there, watching them stare each other down, until Gooch swings his eyes to me.

"Just don't wrestle her off today," he says. "Let her have three matches."

LaRocca shrugs at me.

After they leave, I wait for my blood to settle. When I emerge into the gym, Rankin raises Bill Robinson's arm in victory. Robinson is all smiles.

The freshman stumbles back to his teammates. Guys slap his hand.

Rankin announces, "One thirty-eight, you're up."

I pull on my headgear and snap the chinstrap. I tell myself that I owe her nothing. After all, Rankin was right about one thing, I really don't know this girl.

Shelby waits in the center circle hopping on her toes, one foot to the other. I am all around larger than her, taller, thicker and bigger in every way. I notice, even in headgear, she's really pretty.

Her handshake is hard and abrupt. Her face a mask of calm.

At the whistle, she circles. Step, foot drag, step, foot drag. I figure I'll wait for her first shot. I snag her wrist. She bats my arm away.

She continues to circle. I focus on her hips and the way she steps to the left. I pass on opportunities for shots and possible takedowns. What am I waiting for? Each of her steps telegraphs her next and leaves her open for shots. Too much movement is as bad as too little. What was it my coach used to say, *Be the snake, not the rabbit.*

I lock arms with her, push forward and feel my strength and weight advantage. I secure an inside position and force her hands onto my shoulders. She tries to slide in low for a single-leg. I slip my arm behind her neck and work it into an inside collar. I tug her in close, bringing our heads, ear to ear.

"Let me win."

I freeze.

"Three matches," she breathes. "Then it's yours."

Still processing her words, I take her down to the mat and work the move into two points.

Let me win?

Gooch was telling the truth?

She lies on her stomach, arms outstretched. I'm over her. Shelby tightens her back muscles. Still stuck on her three words, *Let me win,* I decide to let her up. She earns a point.

I face her.

"Come on, Mike," growls Rankin. "Showcase some of those skills."

She comes at me for a single. I step back and trap her in a headlock. She tries to drive forward, maybe force me out of bounds. I'm not moving.

Let me win.

I pivot on my front toe and turn hard, jamming my hip

across her body. Even before she's flying over my back, I know I have her. One second she's on her feet, the next she's soaring head over heels. She lands flat on her back, one arm caught under me, the other slapping the mat.

Her legs twist, her body bucks and flops. With my weight on her chest, leveraged with my splayed legs, I tighten my headlock into a vise. The pin is a matter of leaning hard on her right shoulder and trapped arm. Red faced, fighting, spit on her mouthpiece, eyes round as nickels, she gulps air. With the win coming, a surge of adrenalin floods my muscles.

Guys are cheering, yelling, "Florida! Florida!"

I don't want to feel anything for her. I wipe my mind clean and go for the pin.

Rankin drops flat out on the mat. For an old man, he moves fast. His hand slides under Shelby's shoulder blades. I tighten the hold. My bicep is full in Shelby's face, contorting her lips and nose. I rise higher on my toes and peer down at her face. Her wide eyes are burning with outrage. I have never felt sorry about pinning anyone, until today. Still, I can't imagine the tables turned, me on my back, her squeezing a headlock. No, I could never let her win.

Rankin slaps the mat and sounds his whistle signaling the pin.

I release her and hop to my feet. I am sweating and breathing hard.

Guys are cheering, clapping, yelling, "Florida."

I extend my hand to Shelby. Face flushed, cheeks glowing, she ignores me, rips off her headgear.

My eyes search the team's faces for Gooch and land on Principal Hoffman. He's standing against the wall with his arms folded. His face is tight as a fist. His eyes burn into Shelby's back as she walks slowly to the girls' locker room.

Chapter 7

I DREAM that my mother is in my aunt's front yard smoking a cigarette. She's wearing her favorite tight Levi's and my father's old plaid CPO jacket with the collar flipped. The gray sky is misting rain. Leaves blow across the yard from a stiff wind. "Ma, it's cold," I say. "Come in the house."

Tears spill down her cheeks. "Why did you leave me?" she cries. "Why?"

"You told me to go."

"But you never listened to me."

I jolt awake.

Somewhere in the house, a television plays the morning's news. The rich aroma of my aunt's coffee swims in the air. My heart settles and I call my mother.

"It's me," I say. "I had this weird dream about you."

"Honey, what? I was sleeping."

"It was so real. I think I should come home."

Silence.

She says, "Hold on."

The phone clunks.

A moment later she whispers, "I can talk now, I'm outside

on the steps." I hear the flick of her lighter and the day's first inhale. "Honey," she says, "you promised to give New Jersey a real try."

"No, those are your words," I say. "I only agreed because you were throwing me out."

"I never threw you out," she says. "Did you forget what happened to that boy at school?"

"Do you always have to-." I bite the sentence short. "Mom, what was I supposed to do?"

"What about Jerry's birthday? You did your best to ruin that."

"I told you I couldn't eat cake," I groan. "You knew I was cutting weight for a tournament."

"I gave you a teeny-weenie piece. You could have tasted it," she says. "But instead, what did you do?"

I see the slice of cake stuck to the kitchen wall. Jerry laughed, grinned ear-to-ear and said, *I told you he was a savage. Didn't I tell you?*

"Mom, I shouldn't have thrown the cake. I'm sorry. Is that what you want me to say?"

"You could have apologized to Jerry and you also know that's not why you're in New Jersey."

"Mom, I don't like the way he treats you. I don't even like the way he looks at you."

"He looks at me like a lot of men look at me and someday they won't be looking at all."

"You're my mother."

"You want me to be your mother, then lets talk about your

school work. I was getting phone calls from your teachers. Do you think that's enjoyable?"

"That's only because I didn't want to be in the house with him," I say. "How was I supposed to do my homework?"

"Then let's talk about the last boy you hurt," she says.

I pull the phone from my ear and look at it as if it's become a horrible festering thing. She's making my move to Jersey all my fault? I return the phone to my ear. "Do you have to throw that in my face every time we-."

"It happened Mike." Her words stick like needles. "Don't deny it."

"I know it happened, but it doesn't automatically make it my fault."

"Yes, it does because you were warned and you're the one who hit that boy."

"Stop, Mom. For once can't you be on my side?"

"And pretend you didn't get expelled?"

"Shut up about it!" I shout and end the call.

In my *writing for College* course, last row next to the window, six desks deep, I watch the door for Shelby. Girls, texting or browsing their phones, fill the first two rows across the front of the room. They wear a lot more clothes than the girls in Daytona: stretchy jeans or black tights tucked into flat-soled Uggs, shapeless sweaters over pastel long sleeves. Some wear their varsity jackets, or their boyfriend's. Bright patches on the jacket backs announce *GYMNASTICS, TRACK, BAND* and *SWIMMING.*

Guys fill in the middle rows leaving a void around me. As the bell sounds, Shelby zips in with her desert tan GI Jane backpack slung over one shoulder. I'd seen her lugging it through the halls. On the back flap it says *GI Jane -Fighting Human From Head to Toe.*

She plows to the back of the room and halts at the empty desk next to mine. "You mind?" she says and drops her backpack on the floor. As if daring me to object, she slips into the desk.

Like the rest of the class, her thumbs begin flailing away on her phone.

Part of me wants to explain that I had to beat her because I don't wrestle to lose. I'd quit first. Another part of me wants to move to the other side of the room.

My phone buzzes with a text. I'm surprised, it's from Shelby.

- Don't look so bummed - all u did was ruin my life

Is she serious? She's sitting right next to me and sends me this guilt trip? She glances my way and then at her phone.

I type: *don't feel so bad. I had a weight advantage not a fair challenge*

Shelby: *ah duh*

- r u goin to wrestle JV?

Shelby: *like u care*

The teacher, Ms. Campbell, plows down the row. In black tights and a barn-red sweater that can't possibly hide her big butt, she's round as a soup can. She claps her hands, spins and dramatically clears her throat. "Phones away. Time to work. Phones away."

61

Shelby drops her phone in her backpack, moves her hair from her face and turns to me. "For your information, I'm wrestling JV on Wednesday night," she whispers. "But, you probably know, JV never matters. I already have two JV letters and you ended my varsity season."

Her words sting like pellets. I have no idea what to say back because I'm not apologizing for winning.

Ms. Campbell passes out an assignment.

Write an essay on an event in your life, which caused a meaningful change. I tap my pen on my forehead. Should I start with, *When I moved to New Jersey, I ruined a girl's life?*

I sneak Shelby a text.

- Does Campbell read essays 2 class?

Shelby eyes her phone in her backpack, then snatches it.

Shelby: *what's yr meaningful change? kickin my ass? LOL*

I type back: *Yeah LMAO*

I decide to write about my father, about his last deployment to Afghanistan. I've researched the war. I know some facts.

My dad's name was Albert Michael Brooks. He got in the Marines after the World Trade Center blew up. Like me, he was an only child. My mom says he was looking for brothers. In boot camp, he won medals for shooting and physical stuff. When I was two years old, he came home on leave and married my mother on the beach (course, I don't remember this, I was 2 but I saw the wedding photos). My father wore his uniform and most of his buddies were Marines. Then he was sent to Afghanistan. He wrote a lot to my mother and she saved his letters. He was killed with two other guys when a missile hit their armored vehicle.

I stop writing and put down my pen. A fist forms in my throat. I know I should add another paragraph about how my life changed. But, how do I explain that I'll never know if not having a father changed everything, or nothing at all. As a kid I remember my friends' families with dads had a different feeling. There were always plans and projects, while nothing at my house changed. It was always my mom and me and I didn't know how to fix it.

I sit back and watch Shelby's tight print fill her paper. Everyone is scratching away except me.

When Ms. Campbell asks if anyone wants to share their essay, the pretty Asian girl, who I've seen at the wrestler's table in the cafeteria and walking with Shelby in the halls, makes her way to the front of the class.

"Go ahead, Janice," says Ms. Campbell.

Her essay begins with the sentence, *My life changed when I was elected the president of the student council for Molly Pitcher High School.*

Guys groan. Phones appear under desktops. Thumbs resume tapping. Janice describes the council's charity work and plans for the coming senior prom.

"Thank you Janice, well done." Ms. Campbell offers an unenthusiastic clap. Shelby and a few others join in.

"Do I have another volunteer?"

Shelby strides to the front of the class, looks at Ms. Campbell and asks, "This is okay, right?"

"The stage is yours," answers Ms. Campbell.

"When I think about my grandma," reads Shelby. "I remember her kindness and gentle voice. She was the rock in my family, the glue that held us all together. She was the person who always knew what was important and what should be forgiven the next morning.

She was born in New Orleans and I mean a long time ago before the Internet, before cell phones, before television, I think. She lived in a place called the 9th Ward. Her parents, five sisters and two brothers lived in a four-room house. My grandmother told me she didn't talk to a white person until she was twelve-years-old. Her first job was shucking oysters for fifty cents an hour. When she was seventeen, she married my grandfather and moved to New York City. She had two sons and they lived in Harlem. One son is my father, the other, my Uncle Henry.

The big change in my life was when my grandmother got pneumonia." Shelby closes her eyes, opens them, then goes on. "She was put in the hospital and died last Thanksgiving. She was sixty-six years old."

Shelby's eyes stay on the paper. "I miss her every day. My house is quieter now and not fun. I do remember all the things she taught me, like how to bake rhubarb pie and how to stay proud and remember my African-American heritage."

The class is quiet. Shelby dips her head and returns to her desk.

Chapter 8

ON WEDNESDAY NIGHT, parents are scattered across the bleachers. Most of them are eyeballing their phones. Little kids in street clothes chase each other around the gym in a game of tag. JV Minutemen perform stretches in mismatched sweats and singlets, while two dads act as refs on the center mat. The electronic time clock over the basketball nets isn't even turned on. In Daytona, JV wore nice uniforms and wrestled before varsity. Here, in Molly Pitcher, they are definitely treated like the second string. Obviously, Mr. Goochinov only supports the varsity team.

Shelby warms up at the edge of the sprawl with her legs out straight, holding the soles of her wrestling shoes. She touches her forehead to her large black kneepads and holds the stretch. She's not wearing her varsity singlet. Instead, she wears a plain black one.

"Hey," I say.

She raises her eyes, blinks, studies my face.

I try to come up with something clever and blurt, "What's tonight's order?"

"The order?" she repeats.

"Yeah, when are you wrestling?"

She lets me hang there, not saying a word.

Seconds drag by. "Look about wrestle-off-."

Her eyebrows shoot up. "Forget it."

"Good, I will," I say.

I do feel sorry about her not having a varsity season. Of course, I'm not going to tell her.

She goes back to stretching, alternately tapping her forehead on her kneepads. "And stop looking at me like I'm supposed to apologize."

"I'm not."

"You don't need my approval to wrestle on varsity."

My chest feels like it's about to explode. "Really, because I don't want it."

"Then what are you doing here?" she says.

I shrug, jam my hands in my pockets and try to think of some snappy comeback. "Thought I'd catch some wrestling."

She rolls her eyes. "Yeah, right."

Still, I don't move.

She holds her forehead like she has a headache. "Look, Mike, I don't blame you for anything. I'm sorry I said that during our match. I was feeling desperate. If you could keep that on the down-low."

"Of course."

"Maybe you did me a favor. If I'd stayed on varsity my season would have been trash anyway. How am I supposed to wrestle up a weight class? You fixed everything for me. Problem solved. So enjoy varsity. Win some matches for the team. I'll be rooting for you."

I ask, "What did you weigh tonight?"

"One thirty one."

"You ever think about wrestling off Gooch?"

"You mean again?"

"Yes, again."

"Yeah of course I've thought of it." She shuts her eyes tight. "Look, it's complicated. Gooch and I..., he..." She doesn't go on.

I squat beside her. "I could teach you some moves. Put a game plan in your head."

"Stop, you're forgetting something. Being on varsity means a lot to Gooch. Do you think I'm going to wake up tomorrow and be so much better that..." Again, she doesn't go on. Her eyes freeze on someone or something across the gym.

I follow her gaze to her father, dressed casually in jeans and a short canvas jacket. He's shaking Mr. Goochinov's hand. "What's Gooch's dad doing here?"

"There are things you don't know and don't understand," she says.

"Like what?"

"Like how about Gooch's father owns the restaurant where we have our wrestling dinner. Guess what the dinner costs the wrestlers?"

"Nothing?"

"You get a lollipop," she says like a wiseass.

I return to the bleachers, climb to the top row and check the time. I still have to get back to the gym to clean the locker room.

I put my hands on my cheeks and sink my elbows into my knees. On the other side of the gym, Shelby talks to her father. Tall and wide shouldered, the principal makes her look undersized, almost puny. He says something in her ear. Chewing her mouthpiece, she nods and tugs up her kneepads.

The first JV match at 126 pounds ends after three periods. The Mustang wrestler raises his arm in victory and smiles proudly. Two people, I guess his parents, stand and clap. The mom shouts, "Way to go Scotty."

The 132-pound Mustang wrestler jogs to the center circle and bounces on his toes. He's short, muscular, and, like Shelby, carries most of his weight and strength in his hips and legs. By the look of his smooth cheeks and baby face, I figure he's a ninth grader, maybe tenth.

A dad playing "ref," calls the wrestlers in. Shelby shakes her opponent's hand and they square off on the mat in neutral position.

At the whistle, Shelby, knees bent, hands at the ready, steps in a circle. Her opponent begins a slow stalk. Each time he reaches for her wrist, she pushes his arm away. I wonder if this is part of her strategy. I doubt it. To me, it looks like a bad habit. The Mustang wrestler shoots, snags her ankle and kicks out her support leg. Shelby breaks her fall with her hands. The Mustang wrestler slides behind her for an easy takedown.

The ref raises two fingers.

Principal Hoffman yells, "Come on Shelby, wake up!"

The Mustang wrestler tries to turn her onto her back. There are at least a half dozen ways to accomplish this. He chooses the first move every wrestler learns, a half nelson. He locks his arm behind her neck and swings his body over and across hers. His weight twists her torso and lifts her hips off the mat. He leans hard and cranks her shoulders, but can't completely flip her over.

Because there is no buzzer, someone flings a rolled-up towel onto the mat, signaling the end of the period.

The Mustang wrestler's tilt of Shelby's shoulders earned him three points. She's behind five to nothing.

Second period, the Mustang wrestler has the choice to start in neutral position or referee's position. He chooses the top-referee's position. Shelby gets on her hands and knees. The Mustang wrestler wraps his arm on her waist and grips her elbow.

The whistle sounds.

Shelby pops up and separates, earning one point for her escape.

They circle.

Her father's voice booms across the gym. "Take a shot! Come on Shelby, shoot!"

She shoots.

Her opponent sprawls, trapping her beneath him. He scoots around behind her and earns two points for another takedown. Shelby falls behind seven to one. The score is getting out of reach.

The match goes on like this. Shelby missing opportunities, taking wishy-washy shots.

Her father's barrage of instructions continues, "Tie up.

Move. Stay on your toes."

After three periods, she loses ten to three.

I have one initial thought in my head – I did her a favor. If she'd stayed on varsity, she would have been massacred. I know that much for sure.

I rinse the mop and fill the bucket with steaming hot water. I clean like someone possessed. Working at triple speed, I whip the mop around the floor, under the sinks and into the toilet stalls.

Tony's voice echoes over the loud speakers, "The club will be closing in thirty minutes, please plan your workouts accordingly."

I finish the mirrors and head to the weight room to get in a few sets of bench, and stack and rack the loose weights. Tony added this assignment saying it would only take a few minutes. As I slide 45-pound plates onto an Olympic bar, my eyes screech to a stop. Shelby is across the weight room next to the lat pull-down machine.

The thump, thump of my heart starts in my chest. I cross to her and say, "I almost didn't see you over here."

She lifts her gaze from her phone. Two identical mother-of-pearl dragonfly barrettes hold her hair from her face. Her right cheek is red and puffy.

"I suck, don't I?" she says. "I do, admit it."

"No, you didn't look bad," I lie. "Are you okay?"

She touches her cheek. "I keep asking myself why. Why am I wrestling if I can't win a stinking JV match?" She sighs. "Want to hear what my father's said?"

I wait.

"He said I don't want it bad enough, said I don't try hard enough. Said I might as well quit if my heart isn't in it." She wipes a tear from her eye. "With him it's win or nothing. He lives by three rules." She raises her index finger. "One, effort is within the athletes' zone of control." Her middle finger goes up, "Two, success is giving everything you have and three, his most important rule, never ever give up." She tries to laugh and a tear streaks her cheek. "My mother thinks he's too hard on me, but the truth is, sometimes I don't know how bad I do want it." She slides down the wall mirror until her knees are under her chin. "In the beginning my dad liked the idea of me wrestling. You know, me being tough and doing a boy's sport, like it set me apart. But once I started losing, he wanted me back on volleyball."

"He sounds totally intense," I say.

She half smiles. "He says he doesn't care if I win and at the same time he expects me to win. That's the way he lived his life. In the NFL, you were either extra-ordinary or you were gone. He is always trying to prove something. My father is the only African American principal in the school district. Every day he proves he's up to the job, that he is more than a two hundred and forty pound football player."

"And your mother?" I ask. "What does she think about your wrestling?"

"She worries about me not being as strong as the boys. Thinks I'm going to get hurt. She even worries about me having my period and embarrassing myself. Like she never heard of tampons, like I wouldn't be aware of this. She doesn't understand how a girl could like wrestling. She thinks the boys are looking at my ass and groping me during practice." She puts air quotes around the word, *groping*. "You ever hear the expression, *All the guys know Amy.*"

I am still stuck on her mention of tampons. I let out a breath and shake my head.

"Well, it means all the guys know *Amy* because when they wrestle *Amy*, they put their hands all over her like it's some kind of make-out session and not a wrestling match. And do you know what the parents said?" she eyes me. "It's not fair to their poor little sons, who only can half wrestle me because they can't put their hands across my chest or between my thighs, like I'm some alien creature, like everything in this world has to be sexual. You ever wrestle a girl?"

"Last year there was this tall girl from Port Orange," I say. "She was a senior and the only girl on her team. I pinned her in twenty seconds."

"What were you thinking?"

"I didn't think it was sexual, if that's what you're asking. I wanted to win, not make-out with her. She did smell better than the guys."

"You see, your little joke, that's what I'm talking about," she says seriously. "On the mat, we don't smell better than the guys. I sweat same as you. I want to be known as a wrestler, that's it. A wrestler."

"Shelby, for me wrestling a girl was no big deal. I wrestled her same as a guy."

"You should tell that to my mother."

I picture it. Shelby coming into her house, storming to her bedroom. Her mother chasing after her, asking if she's okay. Her father yelling, *All I ask is that you try.*"

"If I win, I'm the golden girl until I lose, and as you now know, I lose a lot," she sniffles, finds a tissue in her sweatshirt pocket and wipes her nose. "And next week, if I was wrestling varsity I'd be facing Vladimir Roister. He's this totally stripped-out Russian on the Red Devils and then there's Andrew Fox on the Trojans. He's Jersey's wrestling superstar. Won the States as a freshman and every year after. He's an undefeated senior. Can you guess his weight class?"

"138?"

Shelby half whispers, "So now you have to wrestle the great Andrew Fox and I don't."

I shrug.

She asks, "You're not worried?"

"I've won big matches and lost them. I try not to let it get to me."

"Yeah, right," cracks Shelby. "Wait until you check out Roister. He's jacked to the max."

"Wrestling is what I don't worry about."

"That's because you don't have a father with his own memorabilia room." She watches my face. "I'm sorry that didn't come out right."

"Don't worry, I never knew my father, not really. If it weren't for photos, I wouldn't even know what he looked like."

"My dad told me he died in Afghanistan."

"Blown up," I say. "What they found of him is buried in Arlington National Cemetery." I picture my father's single white cross in the sea of crosses.

Her face beats with blood. "I'm really sorry."

"What else did your father tell you about me?"

"I don't know," she says. "Nothing much."

I wonder if she knows about my fights or my nickname. I squeeze my hands into fists. My coach once told me I have stonemason hands and boxers' wrists. He said my "grip strength" was my best weapon on the mat. I'd like to tell Shelby that my last fight, the one that bought my ticket to Jersey, wasn't my fault. I picture Kyle Scruggs surrounded by his friends, all of them chanting, fight, fight, fight. A tremor passes over my shoulders.

"The school files," I say with the words feeling heavy as dumbbells, "they are confidential, right?"

"Oh, of course," she answers quickly.

I want to believe her. "Because, New Jersey is like a new start for me," I say. "I want certain things to stay in Florida."

Tony's second announcement booms through the empty gym. "Work-Out-World is now closed."

"Come on, Mike," says Shelby in a light voice. "I'm not judging you." She looks at me straight on. Under the gym lights, her skin is a beautiful deep woody brown.

I ask, "Are you wrestling for you or for your father?"

She thinks a moment. "I suppose some part of me does everything for my parents. A larger part is trying to prove something, maybe to him. I don't know."

"Prove what?"

"You don't want to hear this."

"I do."

"Just that I'm for real and I'm good enough. I know guys on the team think I'm trying to get attention, like look at her, the only girl and not only that, the only African American. That's not it at all. I'm wrestling because I like it. I like the sprawling, standing up again, the sprints, getting ready for battle. It's hardcore. It keeps me in shape and it's what I want to do. I'm also trying to show everyone, even my mother, that I'm not so delicate, that I'm as tough as anyone whoever stepped on a wrestling mat."

"I think if you dropped some bad habits you'd win more matches."

"And then what? I'll never beat you at 138 and I can't wrestle-off Gooch again."

"Why not?"

"I told you, it's complicated."

"Complicated how?"

"Gooch is the only one on the team that never treated me like the enemy. I'm not saying he isn't a jerk sometimes, but that's just him. He can't help it. Maybe part of me wanted to lose my wrestle-off with Gooch. I knew 138 was open, so we both found a niche."

"You call *him* wrestling at his actual weight class and *you* losing your matches at 138 a niche?"

She makes this smacking noise with her lips like it's so

obvious. "In case you haven't noticed, I'm a girl. Parents don't want me on the team. In my freshman year, they actually talked about hiring an attorney to get me thrown off. So this year, when I filled an empty weight class, they had less to bitch about."

"Sounds like you're making excuses," I say.

"For who?"

"Yourself."

"You say that because you never lost to a girl. You don't know how it feels. Supposedly, it's not good for the male ego. I beat this one boy last year. He was so stressed over losing to me, a girl, that he quit his team. Some of the girl wrestlers I know have started blogs. They post their videos of wins over the boys. It's getting to be a war."

The gym is a tomb. I listen to the silence. Tony will be locking the doors.

"After I challenged Gooch and lost, he took 132 and everything settled down," she says. "I wrestled at 138 and Rankin avoided a team forfeit. Gooch's father had already agreed to fund the Minutemen. He's paying for everything: uniforms, Rankin's extra-curriculum salary, even the bus to our away matches. If Gooch had to wrestle 138, he'd probably quit. If he quit, his father would be spending a lot of money on a team that didn't include his son." She watches my face. "I know, it's totally warped. But, Molly Pitcher isn't a big town. The school district only funds five sports and wrestling isn't one of them."

"What about your father?" I ask. "Can't he go to the school

board or something?"

"He tried and he'll try again next school year. This year, Mr. Goochinov became a voting member of the school board, so wrestling will probably get funded."

"I've wrestled Gooch at practice. I think you could beat him. Maybe not now, but with some training."

Shelby's lip curls up on one side. She pushes my shoulder. "With your top secret methods?"

I ask, "What were you thinking when you stepped on the mat tonight?"

"Thinking?"

"Yeah."

"The truth?" she asks. "I was thinking I'm going to be sick."

"Why?"

"That guy was built like an ATM."

"He was," I agree, "but all he had over you was his weight. You have experience and mat time."

Shelby looks at me like I'll never understand her predicament and takes a pull from her water bottle.

"Really," I say. "Being a senior gives you a monster advantage. You just have to get your head right. My old coach taught us a way to prepare for matches. He called it *Think Wrestling*. First rule - believe you can win. Second, - always have a plan. Third - visualize your win."

"You're going to lecture me?" she groans. "If I wanted a lecture, I could have stayed home."

"You kept pushing your opponent's hand away. Why? What's that about?"

"I don't know. That's the way I wrestle."

"You could have grabbed his wrist, pulled him off balance and taken a clean shot."

"I took shots. You saw what happened."

"Your shots weren't clean. You shoot and then hesitate, like you've changed your mind. You might as well hold up a sign saying, *I'm going to shoot.*"

"Now you sound like my father."

"Did your father notice it too?"

"No, he just delivers all these wisdom bombs, like he's so much wiser than anyone on the planet. He constantly tells me to stay off my back." She laughs. "Like when I have a one hundred and twenty-eight pound guy on me, cranking me over with my face in his hairy armpit, it's so easy."

I laugh. I'm tempted to take her hand, want to, but don't move. "You did some good things on the mat. You earned that escape. He couldn't hold you."

"I'm good at getting out from the bottom position."

"That's part of *Think Wrestling*," I say with some excitement. "You believed you could do it and it happened."

A small smile appears on her face.

"Shelby, I can show you ten basic moves and some pinning moves," I say. "My coach in Daytona believes all a wrestler needs is ten moves."

She rises and turns to the mirror, wipes her eyes, touches the bruise on her cheek. "I think I should quit."

"If you don't love it," I say honestly. "You should."

She faces me.

I am only about three inches taller than her. My skin is buzzing, fingertips tingling from her heat.

"Do you love it?" she asks.

"I just don't want to know what I'd be if I weren't a wrestler."

"How about your normal good guy in the eleventh grade."

"I doubt that," I say. "Maybe if I grew up here, but not in Daytona. Everyone was put in these groups, the surfers, the stoners, the partiers, the brains, the Richie Richards."

"What's a Richie Richard?"

"You know, the kids with a terminal case of affluenza."

"What group were you in?"

"My own group, the wrestlers," I say without thinking.

She insists on driving me home. The night is cold and damp. The air feels wet. We walk to her car at the end of the lot. Her Honda Civic has a slamming stereo. She cranks *Pink* until the bass pulses like a heartbeat. Heavy on the gas, she cuts the corner of the gym's parking lot and speeds along Molly Pitcher Road.

I ask, "How long have you had your driver's license?"

She smiles and abruptly brakes at a stop sign sending her gym gear off the back seat. "About two weeks." She laughs. "What about you?"

I don't want to explain that I was disqualified from my driver's test because my mother's minivan side mirror is held on with duct tape and doesn't adjust. Jerry said fixing it would cost more than the van was worth. I was supposed to borrow a car from a neighbor, but he changed his mind at the last minute.

"I think you make a right turn here," I say.

"You think?" she laughs. "You don't know where you live?"

We zip through the night, past lit-up houses, some with early Christmas lights twinkling on bushes and rooflines. Streets curve one into the other. The little Honda's tires grip the road and the music seems to propel us along.

In front of my aunt's house, she pulls to the curb, puts the car in park and lowers the volume on the radio.

"I love this car," she says. "It's small but it kicks ass, doesn't it?"

I tell her it's faster than it looks.

"My father bought it for me, sort of a 'Hey, thanks for being a good kid' present. Have you Googled him yet?" She faces me in her bucket seat. "Bruce Wallace Hoffman?"

I hadn't.

She tells me about his seven years in the NFL and his career ending knee injury, "...a torn ACL. He couldn't come back from it. Now he's developed arthritis in the joint. You know, there's a connection between a torn ACL and osteo-arthritis."

I didn't know it. Had never even heard of osteo-arthritis.

"After football, he taught phys ed, coached the football team, then went back to school and got a masters in administration. He's been the principal at Molly Pitcher for two years." Enthusiasm fades from her eyes. "Which if you want to know the truth, sucks for me. If I skip a homework, he knows about it before I do. He's also up on the school's gossip. You'd be surprised how much the teachers talk. There was this one girl, who thought she was pregnant and swore me to secrecy.

That same night I heard my father telling my mother about a guidance counselor providing the girl with a pregnancy test."

"Was she pregnant?"

"No, false alarm or at least that's the edited for TV version."

In the moon lit car, I watch her straight teeth and jewel green eyes flash as she speaks with urgency, like everything is remarkable. For the second time that night, I contemplate taking her hand.

"I have a little brother," she says. "He's on the Molly Pitcher Musketeers. It's full uniform, contact, tackle football. My father videos his games. He critiques every play."

"How old is he?"

"Eleven. I love him, but he's such a pain and a wise ass. You wouldn't believe." She rolls her eyes. "Always taking my stuff, always tattling and wanting me to screw up."

When she moves her hand to the console, I inch my fingers closer to hers. She goes on about her brother. I am barely listening. I make minute advances toward her hand until I take it in mine. I can feel her heartbeat, or imagine I can feel it.

I don't move, don't breathe. She lets her hand linger and I'm thinking about kissing her.

"Wow it's late," she exclaims and turns back to the steering wheel. "I still have chemistry homework."

We say a rushed goodbye. In the next moment, I'm watching her tail lights grow faint and out of sight.

Chapter 9

SATURDAY, I arrive at the high school in the thin rays of dawn's cold first light. It's the first match of the season and there's no way I was going to be late. I chain my aunt's bike to the rack behind the school at the edge of the baseball diamonds, cross the teacher's parking lot and trot up the stairs to the gym doors. I give each door handle a pull. All locked.

I wait on the concrete steps thinking about last night. How could Shelby be hung up on Gooch? He's such a little conniving prick. I already suspect that he snatched my towel in the locker room and threw it into the showers. I had to stand naked under a hand dryer. After I dressed, I grabbed Gooch by the back of the neck and pulled him into a bathroom stall. "You ever do that again," I whispered. "I'll flush your head down that toilet."

All he said was, "Dude, you should get some professional help." Like he's so funny, so self-righteous. I was hoping he'd at least push me.

A pickup truck rumbles past and parks. Coach Rankin in his Saturday jeans and parka steps out and crosses the lot.

"You early," he grunts to me. "Me like early. Early good." He smiles. "That's my cave man impression. What's the matter, you don't like it?"

Despite myself, I smile and follow him into the school.

The locker room is deserted. I strip to my briefs and socks and step onto the scale. I'm 142, four over. Last night, I had three freakin' turkey meatballs for dinner and then starved the rest of the night! My aunt told me the meatballs were low calorie, one hundred percent white meat turkey.

"What's the verdict?" asks Rankin from the doorway.

I mumble, "I'm a few over."

"I know what a couple is, but what's a few?" The coach comes along side and sees the number. "Too much salad?" he asks and laughs at his joke.

"I wish."

"I'm sure you know the drill. Get on the bike, then hit the track. You got sweats?"

I nod.

"Put them on, tops and bottoms with the hood up. One more thing, did you have a bowel movement today?"

"A what?"

"A number 2?"

I hesitate, "Ah, no. Not yet."

"Then think about having one. Go lie on the mat and throw your legs over your head. It's a Yoga move, called, plow pose. Look it up on your phone. You do have a dumb phone?"

"You mean a smart phone."

"No, a dumb phone because all you kids do is text and

83

Instagram all day and obliterate the English language."

I laugh. "Then yeah, I have a dumb phone."

"Good, Google plow pose. Stay crunched over like that for five minutes."

Uncomfortable with the subject, I step off the scale.

"Don't look so mortified," smiles Rankin. "We're all human. We have that in common. It's the homeostatic processes of osmoregulation and excretion. You want to know the difference, stop by some time and we'll talk. I used to teach biology. You didn't know that, did you?" He grabs my shoulder and shakes it. "Thirty five years, loved every minute of it. But, things change, administrations change. Now I'm Driver's Ed and Detention." The Coach glances at me like he expects me to say some wise crack.

"I guess you miss teaching bio," I say.

He nods. "You guys are the last good thing I'm holding on to. Now get dressed and don't forget, bike, track, plow pose and not necessarily in that order."

When the national anthem ends, the crowd of parents and students clap and whistle. Some one yells, "Let's wrestle!"

I remove my hand from my heart. I made weight. Plow pose, bike and a two-mile jog did the trick. I look for Shelby. She's in street clothes, wearing these really tight black corduroy's cuffed around her ankles and Nike Air Force 1 sneakers. She looks awesome.

She catches me watching her and jogs across the mats. "I'm helping Janice keep the clock," she says. "My first time."

First time because I put you on JV, I think.

She peers over at the Mustangs milling around their folding chairs. "You're wrestling Russo, the short guy with the tats," she says.

My eyes settle on a barrel-chested wrestler with smeary-inked arms and bulky muscles.

"I wrestled him last season," she says. "Unorthodox style. Like completely erratic, but good on his feet. I should have won. He caught me in a cradle."

I never liked wrestling short guys. They're hard to shoot on. Hard to move around the mat.

"Will you be at Work-Out-World tonight?" she asks.

"I'm at the gym every night," I say.

"You think you could show me some moves? I mean, if you still want to." Her voice is unsure. "Might be fun to win a few JV matches this season." She releases a strained laugh.

"Definitely." I try not to look too pleased.

She jogs back to the scoring table.

Coach Rankin appears out of nowhere. His face is set solid as cement. "We need to talk," he says.

"Something wrong?" I ask.

"Come on, in my office."

I follow the coach through the parents and kids. He flips his office lights on. "I have to tell you something," he says glumly. "And, you're not going to be happy."

I wait holding the back of a chair.

He asks, "How old are you?"

"Seventeen."

"When's your birthday."

"August eighth."

"You wouldn't lie to me?"

"No."

Rankin runs his hands over his thinning hair. "The Mustangs filed a petition. They're challenging your status on the Minutemen. Apparently your school file doesn't contain your birth certificate. Not even a copy or a scanned document. I'm sorry, but you can't wrestle today. We'll get the paperwork straight and you'll wrestle next week."

I keep my eyes on the coach. I'm still not completely getting it. "So they think I'm older than seventeen?"

"They claim that you turned nineteen before the start of the season, which equals disqualification."

"No way. I'm in eleventh grade. Did you tell them that?"

He nods gravely.

"And how would the Mustangs know what's in my file?" I ask.

The coach doesn't move for a second. The sagging skin under his neck twitches like a pulse. "That I don't know. Still, the bottom line is the league officials decided the issue has to be resolved before you wrestle."

"It's got to be Principal Hoffman," I spit.

Coach Rankin puts his hand on my shoulder. "Now don't start accusing people. We'll get this cleared up."

I sit on the sideline watching Shelby warm up for *my* match.

Mine. Shining and sleek in her varsity singlet, she has transformed into a wrestler. Her makeup and earrings are gone. Her hair is tucked under a skullcap. She reminds me of a young super hero, think Halle Berry when she played Storm in X-Men. The guys on the other team are checking her out and passing whispers. I'd like to talk to her, but her father is on her like a hired bodyguard.

The full implications continue to hit me like slaps across the face. How could anyone know my birth certificate wasn't in my file unless Principal Hoffman was in on it? Why else would the other team challenge my age? My face is red-hot, skin glowing with outrage.

Dustin and LaRocca come along side me.

"Everybody's saying you're like thirty-five years old," laughs Dustin.

"Well, I'm not."

"Still," he says. "I heard about this dude that entered a tournament and said he was eighteen. He won and it came out that he was twenty-two. He had all this bogus ID."

LaRocca shakes his head at Shelby. "It's too bad," he says. "Cuz Shelby can't beat Russo. We all know that."

"Be cool," I say. "She'll hear you."

"Let her hear me," says LaRocca. "That's the problem, isn't it? Everyone treating her special, acting like we owe her something because she's a girl."

I push LaRocca in the chest. "Just shut up."

"Look at you," he says. "Benched and still taking her side."

I slam out the gym doors into the hall. I think about leaving the school, just saying the hell with all of it.

"I hope you're not blaming me."

I turn around. It's Shelby in her singlet and wrestling shoes.

"Why would I? It wasn't your fault."

"My father was as surprised as me. The coach on the other team lodged a challenge. Claims he has a right to ask for your birth certificate."

"And I suppose your father had nothing to do with it and always tells you the truth," I say.

A frown wrinkles her forehead. "He's a lot of things, but not a liar," she says. "If you don't believe me, fine. Everyone in this school blames my father for something."

"Shelby, I'm sorry. I believe you."

She shrugs off my apology. "Do you really think he'd risk his reputation so that I could wrestle Russo? I'm only a hundred and thirty pounds today and he's even more jacked than last year."

"Muscles don't win wrestling matches," I say. "Russo's got to be freaking out right now."

"And why's that?"

"Because he's no different than every guy here. He doesn't want to lose to a girl. Believe me."

"Just because I'm a girl?"

I stare at Shelby's pretty face trying to sort things out. "Yeah, think about it. How is losing to you going to make him feel?"

"All right, so he's going to wrestle me tough," she says. "How does that help me?"

"He'll make mistakes and take more risks. You've got to be

aggressive. If it's a close match don't watch the clock. Wrestle hard until the whistle. If you're ahead, use the clock, otherwise it doesn't exist."

"My problem is going to be his strength," she says.

"When you're in bottom position don't try to stand straight up." I think a moment. "How's your sit-out-and-turn?"

She shrugs. "Pretty good."

"It's got to be better than pretty good."

"It's solid," she says.

"When you're on the bottom, imagine your legs as two sticks of dynamite. At the whistle, explode into the sit-out, then bam, explode into the turn. The second turn is where everyone gets caught. They only explode once. Keep thinking of two sticks of dynamite. Two separate explosions."

"Okay," she says. "I can do that."

"If you're on top, he's going to be hard to hold down. Soon as the whistle blows, start pushing forward on your toes so that he can't get a foothold. Ride him out of bounds. Don't let him get upward momentum. Am I making sense?"

Thinking, she nods. "What else?"

"When you take a shot, imagine you're shooting through him, not at him, through him, like you're shooting into a long tunnel and only have one chance to go the entire distance. Don't hesitate. You decide to shoot, it's go time. There's only one way to daylight and it's straight through him."

She nods. "Okay, I can do that."

"If you shoot for a single-leg and have it but can't budge him, work your arms up his body and then lean back and throw him."

"No way, not with his weight advantage," she says.

"Then try a fireman's carry. We practiced it, remember?" Her eyes give me the feeling that she's about to lean in and kiss me.

"Thanks, Mike," she says. "I better get warmed up."

The match opens with Russo pushing Shelby around. He muscles her to her knees and tumbles on top of her. It's a terrible start. I can hardly watch.

Takedown Russo. Two points.

Somehow Shelby escapes his grip and earns a point. They tie up, each of them pushing and pulling, trying to set up a shot. Shelby dives for his legs. She's in on his ankle, but can't move him. Like she said, he's too heavy. She releases and tries to find an exit.

Over the cheers from the stands, Principal Hoffman shouts, "Get inside, get inside."

Coach Rankin smacks a rolled paper on his thigh and booms, "Head high, lower your hips."

Shelby looks like a rag doll in the jaws of a bulldog. Russo is shoving her around the mat. Principal Hoffman yells, "Do something. Make something happen!"

Doesn't her father know Shelby is wrestling up a weight class? She's going to get pushed around. I fold my arms. There is nothing for me to do but watch the slaughter.

Finally, period one ends.

Coach Rankin gives Shelby a thumbs up for top position.

Russo gets on his hands and knees. Shelby drapes herself over him.

At the whistle, Russo is on his feet, towing her around the mat, trying to shake her loose.

The gym explodes with shouts and hoots.

"Don't let go!" yells Principal Hoffman.

Russo unlocks Shelby's grip and earns a point for his escape. They tie up.

Shelby steps in and locks a collar tie around Russo's neck. She gets a grip on his left arm.

I see the move happening before it happens. She lowers to one knee, her right arm slips between his legs, her other arm holds his wrist tight. She begins to turn him like the blade of a windmill. It's a perfect fireman's carry, until she stalls midway and Russo comes down on top of her.

The gym bursts with excitement. Russo is chest to chest with her. Shelby, on her back, arches in a high bridge, rocks side to side, throwing her legs right and left. Finally, her bridge collapses. She's flat on her back squirming, trying to get out of bounds.

I check the clock. Forty seconds.

The Mustang's coach yells, "Lift the head, lift the head."

Russo is crushing her. He leans back, pulling her head up. Shelby seems to lose her will or concentration, or maybe she's exhausted, simply too tired to fight.

The ref's hand slaps the mat. Pin!

Russo leaps to his feet and raises his arms in victory.

She flips over, gets to her knees and stands. She shakes

Russo's hand and wanders toward her father on the sidelines. Her dad's face wears her loss. It's not a look of devastation, but one of complete frustration.

"What the hell do you call that?" he roars.

Chapter 10

I'M CHILLIN' on the floor in my mom's old room, listening to her CDs on her ancient boom box, when a call comes in just before ten at night. I don't recognize the number and almost don't answer because I've been getting bombarded with spam from some travel agency telling me I've won a trip to St. Croix.

I pick up.

It's Shelby.

"You get a new phone?" I ask, surprised.

"Nah, it's my parent's landline. They're like from the stone ages. They think if the world ends and all the cell towers crumble to the ground, they'll still be able to call for take-out."

I crawl across the floor and kill the music.

"Today sucked," she says.

"You almost had him."

"I know, that's the worst part of it."

"It was like you changed your mind halfway into the fireman's carry."

"Don't remind me," she says with annoyance. "I've watched it twice. My dad's watched it twenty times."

"What happened?"

"I suppose I panicked. I kept thinking he was going to squash me, you know with all his weight, and then he did." She laughs sadly. "Believe it or not, my brother and I had been practicing the Fireman's carry."

"Where?"

"We have a mat in the basement. My dad plays coach. He'll watch a move on YouTube and think he's an expert on it. Half the time he doesn't know what he's talking about."

I try to visualize Shelby working with her brother as her father leans over them. "Did your father say anything about me?" I ask.

"Only that you have to get your original birth certificate."

"That's it."

"Basically, yeah."

My door opens. Auntie's head pokes in. She's wrapped her hair in cellophane. I can smell her hair-dye chemicals.

I wave the phone at her.

She disappears, but leaves the door open. I push it shut.

"That was my aunt," I say. "I'm getting used to her, or we're getting used to each other."

"I've watched her lead classes at W-O-W," says Shelby. "She's a great dancer."

"Today she gave me a lecture about bread. Said it isn't a vegetable, said I shouldn't eat more than a slice a day, like I didn't know that."

We laugh.

"I told my dad that you think I should wrestle-off Gooch for

132. He kinda likes the idea."

"Is that what you want?" I picture her wobbling toward her father after today's match. "Of course, I don't *want* to wrestle-off Gooch," she shoots back. "But what other choice do I have?"

I climb onto the bed and lean my back against the wall. "When I was a kid my friends dared me to swim out to a buoy in the bay. I didn't want to do it and I almost drowned."

"And you think that's me?" she asks.

"Maybe."

"Well, you're wrong."

"According to you, he always has your back," I say. "According to him, you're his best friend or something."

She laughs. "Not really."

"What does 'not really' mean?"

"I told you, it's complicated."

"So you're not like seeing him?" I need to hear her say it.

"We have gone out and we still see each other sometimes. Right now, we're just friends."

"Good friends?"

"More like old, good friends," she says.

"You've got to want to beat him," I say. "You can't go out there like B-F-Fs and expect to win."

She is silent for a few seconds, then says, "I can't imagine him on JV."

"Why not?"

"Well, maybe because when anyone in the high school

thinks of Molly Pitcher wrestling, they think of Gooch. He's the team's captain and his father pays for everything."

Another call comes in. My mother. I tell Shelby to hold on.

"I have your birth certificate right here in my hand," exclaims my mother. "It's stamped from the hospital. You're not going to believe where I found it."

I ask, "Where?"

"The glove compartment of the Caravan. How it got in there, I'll never know. I'll get it in the mail tomorrow."

"Certified mail," I say. "If it gets lost I'm screwed."

"Don't worry."

I tell her I've got to go and click back to Shelby. She's no longer there. I drop the phone on my bed and find my aunt in the kitchen. She's rinsed her hair.

"My mother has my birth certificate," I say. "She's mailing it tomorrow."

My aunt extends her arms. By now I know the drill and walk into them. She squeezes me tightly. "I told you it would be okay," she says. "By the way, I was talking to your mother last night. She told me something I didn't know." She pulls out a chair. "Have a seat."

I slide in and she sits across from me.

"Can we talk, honestly?" She reaches across the table and brushes the back of her fingers on my cheek. "Tell me why you left Daytona."

"Didn't my mother tell you?"

"I want to hear it from you."

I blow out breath.

"You can't run from yourself," she says.

"It was stupid," I say. "It's like too stupid to even talk about."

"Try me."

"You know you're really annoying sometimes," I say.

She gives me an amused twist of her lips. "That might be true. But, it doesn't change anything. So, why are you here in New Jersey? Tell me."

"Well," I say. "You know about Jerry. We didn't get along. I didn't like the way he treated my mother."

"But you put up with Jerry for two years," she says. "And supposedly your mother likes him."

"Yes, supposedly."

"What happened at school?"

"A fight."

My aunt's enormous blue eyes wait.

"This football jock, Kyle Scruggs," I say picturing his ugly mug, "he photo-shopped my friend's head onto the cover of *Diary of a Wimpy Kid* and posted it on the school's website. You ever see those books?"

"I've seen them."

"Scruggs is a first class waste of life. He'd been riding my friend since like the fourth grade. He made fun of his clothes, fun of his hair. He left me alone. That just shows you how much of a punk he is. No one messes with the wrestlers."

"You mean, no one messes with Iron Mike," she says.

"My mother told you about that?"

"We were talking and it came up, but go on," she says. "I

shouldn't have interrupted you. Finish your story."

The silence thickens like ice. Her blue eyes wait.

I release a breath. "So my friend didn't play sports and can't fight to save his life. So after the wimpy kid thing, he asked me to talk to Scruggs."

"Talk?" says my aunt skeptically.

"Yeah, talk," I answer fast. "I didn't plan on hitting him."

I picture Scruggs surrounded by his friends, all of them chanting, fight, fight, fight.

"But you did hit him."

"Once," I say.

"Okay, once. Why?"

"Because Scruggs took Taekwondo since he was like five and he started showing off. He snapped a kick in my face. His foot came one inch from my nose and everyone was yelling, trying to get me to fight." A sweat rises from my pores.

"And then what?" she asks

I try to choose my words carefully. "I clocked him."

"With one punch?"

"Yeah."

The sparkle leaves her eyes. "Where did this happen?"

"Behind the school near a duck pond where all the heads smoke weed."

"How did that make you feel?"

"The truth?"

"Yes."

"It made me feel good." I grit my teeth. "Because I get sick of people thinking they can do anything they want to me."

"To you?" she asks. "Don't you mean your friend?"

I don't answer.

My aunt's face remains calm. "This boy Scruggs, he went to the hospital for a broken eye socket?"

I nod.

"How many fights have you been in?" she asks.

"Not that many."

"How many?"

I don't want to tell her, don't want to think about it.

She takes my hand and asks, "How many in the past two years?"

I think about last year's fight in gym class when some kid made fun of my jeans. Somehow I'd sat on a nail that ripped my pants. I suppose you could see my underwear. I should have thrown those pants out. It was another one swing fight. He'd crashed into the lockers and cut his head. I was suspended for a week.

"So how many?" Her eyes wait.

"Maybe five."

"And that's why you were expelled?"

I nod. "Three suspensions is mandatory expulsion."

"What about your mother?"

"What about her?"

"You're angry at her and you've always tried to protect her. That must be hard."

"Don't make it about my mother. Hitting Scruggs and those

kids wasn't about her."

"Underneath it all, I think it's mostly about her. Anger changes people." She leans back and folds her arms like she proved a point.

I'm pissed off and at the same time squinting through watery eyes. I would like to hit something, right there in her kitchen. "Maybe you're right," I say and the voice in my head comes back at me loud. She is right.

Chapter 11

SUNDAY and I don't have to get up. It's my one-day of the week to sleep in. I lie in bed, head propped on my pillow watching Shelby's match with Russo on my laptop. Overnight, someone posted it on YouTube. I watch the video over and over and smile at the look on Russo's face when Shelby spins him through the air. If she just hadn't quit.

My aunt has been up for hours - turning on and off the television, opening and closing doors, maybe rearranging furniture and herding elephants.

I text Shelby:

- *watched the video –it would have been awesome if*

I delete it and type:

- *what ru up 2 today*

I delete that and type:

- *off today, do u want 2 meet @ the gym*

I hit send.

A knock.

"Yeah."

My aunt pushes the door open. She wears a terry cloth bathrobe, slippers and a humongous smile. "Come on," she says. "Sit up and give your aunt a big hug-a-bug."

I don't feel like giving her a hug or a big hug-a-bug.

"Aunt Maggie, I'm not in the best-."

She takes me in her muscled arms. "A hug in the morning turns the day in the right direction," she says in my ear.

Slowly, I put my arms around her.

Still wearing the same big smile, she releases me. I look at her face and see my mother's. They look so much alike, it's almost spooky.

"Okay, here's the plan," she says. "I bought eggbeaters, which are pure egg whites. I cooked some shiitake mushrooms in a light olive oil, full of natural selenium, great for the thyroid, and I could whip that into two beautiful omelets. How does that sound?"

I ask, what selenium tastes like.

She laughs and swipes at my head. "It's a mineral. You don't taste it."

A message pings my phone.

Shelby: *Taking day off, muscles sore - want to meet @ mall @ 2 - some of us r going*

I message back: *sure, where*

Shelby: S*tarbucks*

We walk the mall's lower level, around a globe-shaped fountain. I've barely said two words. I suppose I'm in shock. Somehow, I've been paired off with Janice, the girl in my writing class and president of the student council, while Gooch strolls along with Shelby. I don't know how I'm feeling about it. Betrayed? Scammed? Didn't Shelby open up to me at the gym and then drive me home? Didn't we hold hands? Did I read her all wrong? Is she a tease? I look for an exit door and think about UBERing back to my aunt's house.

The children's train approaches with its fiberglass body and miniature coaches. Some guy in an engineer's hat rings the bell. Janice and Shelby wave and smile as the kids whiz by. At Cinnabon, they snag free samples. Shelby stuffs one in Gooch's mouth. They both crack up laughing. Janice tries to put one in my mouth. I tell her I'm in season.

Watching Shelby and Gooch enjoy each other's company is like listening to a non-stop recording of chalk squeaking on a blackboard. And, this has nothing to do with Janice. Believe me, she's very nice and very pretty. She has this cute outfit thing going on – black stretch peg-leg jeans, a short tan top and cork wedges. But, she's not Shelby.

Gooch talks loudly about some kid that went to a party and drank a bottle of Fireball. "He barfed on the parent's bed, spray-painted it cherry red."

"And when did this happen?" asks Shelby.

"Like two weeks ago?"

Shelby tugs his arm. "You went to a party and didn't tell me?"

Gooch turns around and rolls his eyes at Janice and me. "I bet Florida gets wasted all the time," he says. "Right, Florida?"

I shake my head. "No, I don't."

Showing off for the girls, he blocks my path and makes this stupefied, shocked face. "Wait a minute," he says. "You do drink, don't you?"

103

I don't answer.

Gooch laughs loudly. "Come on, dude, tell us."

I flash on my mother's vodka bottle and the never-ending containers of cranberry juice from Costco. I see her in front of our house, asleep behind the wheel of her car, her foot on the brake, the engine in drive, running all night. The truth is I don't drink and I don't plan on starting.

"No, but I know a lot of complete assholes that do drink," I say.

Gooch smiles and laughs. This guy is unreal. It's like I can't insult him.

"Florida, my man, listen up," he says. "My brother is at college majoring in beer pong with a minor in keg stands. You might as well get your pre-requisites out of the way in high school."

Shelby says, "His name is Mike and why don't you shut up."

"It's cool," I say. "I know plenty of guys like Gooch. He's the dude in a puddle of puke that I step over on New Year's Eve."

It's not meant to be funny, but Janice bursts out in a nervous laugh.

I give Gooch a long look. He's not laughing. I could tell him about my mother's old boyfriend, killed driving drunk. The police found his car flipped over in the Intracoastal Waterway. At the wake someone stuck a bottle of Jack Daniels in the open coffin like it was a big joke.

"It's so obvious," says Gooch. "Florida has never been drunk." He lets out a fake laugh.

The guy is so clueless. It's unbelievable.

"I've seen you wasted plenty of times," says Shelby. "It makes you even dumber than you already are."

"It's supposed to," laughs Gooch. "What's so fun about being sober?"

"Really, you're a Neanderthal," says Shelby. "What's so great about getting drunk and acting like a jerk?"

Gooch takes her hand and pulls her ahead. I fall in step with Janice. We watch them, shoulder-to-shoulder, whisper about something.

"Don't let Gooch get to you," says Janice.

"I don't."

"He always plays the class clown," she says.

Gooch places his arm around Shelby's waist and hooks his finger in the belt loop of her skinny jeans. I can't help noticing they look like a real couple.

"And, it's always been Gooch and Shelby," says Janice. "I can remember going to birthday parties when I was a kid. They'd be dropped off together and picked up like they were brother and sister." Janice slips her arm around mine. "Is this okay?" she asks sweetly.

It hits me like a slow motion punch. Setting me up with Janice is Shelby's way of backing me off.

"I know you like her," says Janice.

I'm sort of glad to hear this news. "She told you that?"

"We talk all the time, like nonstop."

So, I think, Shelby invited me to the mall to show me she's with Gooch, one of the biggest posers I've ever met?

"Do you like her?" asks Janice.

"She's a trip," I say.

"A trip? As in what way?"

"Every way."

"She thinks you like her."

"I didn't say I didn't."

"If she's what you're into," says Janice, removing her arm from mine. "It's fine with me."

"What does that mean?"

Janice tightens her lips. "Nothing."

"No, tell me."

"Try to find five people in the school who think she should be wrestling on a boy's team. Believe me, they don't exist."

"I thought you were on her side."

"I am. I wouldn't be here with you doing her a favor if I wasn't." She gives me a smug smile.

At Victoria's Secret, Janice grabs Shelby's hand. "Time to shop," she says with a mischievous smile.

Gooch tries to say something in Shelby's ear. She laughs and pushes him away.

"Be back," says Janice heading towards racks of negligees and bins of colorful panties and bras.

I think about cutting out, and decide to stay. If nothing else, I'll make Shelby jealous. It's not fair to Janice, but it seems nothing is fair in Molly Pitcher. Gooch follows me to an empty bench under a skylight. I perch on the back of the bench and hunch forward with my new Nike's on the seat. He does the same. Anyone walking by would think we're two bro's, hanging out, shooting the shit. Somewhere speakers are playing an elevator-music version of *Beat It.*

Gooch bongos the edge of the bench and asks, "You find your birth certificate?"

I don't lift my eyes from the terrazzo floor. "It's in the mail."

He sniggers, "Anyone tell you about Vladimir Roister?"

"Yeah, Shelby." I don't tell him I've already done my own research on Roister.

"He won the Districts and the Regions. Last year, he missed the States," says Gooch. "Everyone thought he went back to Russia. Turned out he had ringworm. But, if he'd wrestled, he was a lock for first or second place. So if your birth certificate doesn't arrive by Saturday, Shelby is facing absolute annihilation."

Inside the store, I watch her lift a gigantic bra to her chest and laugh.

"Picture a guy," continues Gooch, "who normally weighs about 152 and cuts to 138. All that's left is this fuming, sucked-out Russian with no neck and a shaved head."

I don't want this garbage stuck in my brain. "You can shut up because you're not going to psyche me out," I say.

"I'm not trying to. Just stating the facts. If I was facing Vladimir Roister, I'd like someone to give me the low down."

I remember this one wrestler from Miami Beach. He somehow got around the rules for cutting weight and routinely cut fifteen pounds for matches. He always fell apart from exhaustion in the 3rd period. I also knew guys that didn't tire out. They went undefeated in high school and then earned full rides to the best colleges.

"Oh, and here's something you and Vladdy have in common," says Gooch. "No one really knows Vladimir Roister's real age. When his family came to America, he didn't have a birth certificate either. Some people think he's twenty-five."

"I have a birth certificate," I say. "And, last time I checked Florida was part of the United States."

Gooch gives a little grin. "What about dentists? Do they have them in Florida."

I feel myself reddening in degrees. "You're a real douchbag," I say. "Aren't you?"

"That was a joke, only a joke."

"We'll see how funny it is in practice," I say.

For once, he doesn't have a response.

I watch Janice pick up a thong from a bin. She looks my way and twirls it.

"Those things can't be comfortable," says Gooch. "I mean, it's a string up your butt crack."

I don't say a word.

"Dude, I was only joking," he says.

I ask, "Is tonight some kind of a double date?"

Gooch chuckles. "I had nothing to do with it."

"I didn't say you did," I say. "But this set up, Janice and me, you and Shelby?"

"Like I said, don't look at me," says Gooch. "If I had to

guess, I'd blame Shelby. She's probably sending you a message. I mean, Florida, we all see the way you look at her. You are so obviously into her and I told you, Shelby and I are tight."

I shut my eyes and take a deep breath.

"Besides, Janice is perfect for you," says Gooch. "Didn't you notice she laughs at everything you say?" He snorts and pantomimes the way Janice wrinkles her nose when she laughs.

I had noticed.

"She likes you," says Gooch. "Consider yourself lucky. Janice is a cool girl. She has an outside shot at being the class valedictorian. You play your cards right and cut your mullet, maybe you'll wind up taking her to the prom. And then who knows what might happen."

"It's not a mullet," I say.

"Man-bun, pony-mullet, whatever," says Gooch.

So I'm with Janice, I think. And, he's obviously with Shelby.

The girls return across the promenade. Each swings a miniature pink shopping bag in their hand.

"What'd you buy?" asks Gooch. "Lemmie see."

"Oh, wouldn't you like to know," says Janice.

The girls giggle.

When Gooch takes Shelby's hand, I feel a wave of nausea.

Janice snags mine and we fall in behind them.

"You okay with this?" she asks, lifting our hands.

I clear my throat, "Sure."

"Do you have a girlfriend?"

I watch Shelby's perfect butt waggle back and forth.

Janice gives me a look, eyes wide, head tilted. "So, do you?"

"No."

At Spencer Gifts, Janice tugs my coat. "Come on, I love this store."

I don't budge.

"Okay then I'll go with Gooch," she says, as if I'm going to be jealous, and follows him into the store.

Shelby stays outside, thumbs working feverishly on her phone. Who could she be texting? A boy? Her mom?

I wander into the GAP and down a row of denim jeans and jackets. Will my new life in Jersey be a series of screwed up dates? How do I accept the fact that I can't have Shelby? I take out my phone and press the UBER app.

When I turn around, she's there.

"Do you like Janice?" She bites her lower lip.

"Was this your idea?"

"You mean you and Janice?"

"Yes, me and Janice."

She asks, "Are you mad?"

"No, but I'm leaving."

"She likes you a lot. She asked me and I figured it would be fun to sort of hang out together."

My heart sinks.

"And, Mike, I will admit, you're a nice guy. We're going to be really good friends, but I am, sort of with Gooch and-."

I feel the blood drain from my head. "What's 'sort of with' mean?"

"You know, off and on. My parents don't want me too serious with any boy."

I step closer to her. Inside my chest, my heart is wild. I don't think I'm reading her wrong. I'm sure she's been flirting with me, Gooch's new enemy.

"Gooch is a clown," I say.

"I know," she agrees, "but-."

"I like you."

"I know you do."

"A lot." My fingers find her hand. Electricity charges up my arm. Thinking about her pillow soft lips, her raspberry lip-gloss and the scent of vanilla in her hair, imagining her hand at the back of my neck, imagining the wave of relief washing over me when I'm finally kissing her, I lean in and it's like I've been waiting for this all my life.

Her hand plants firmly on my chest. "Not yet," she says.

"This isn't okay?" I ask

She squeezes my hand. "Sometime soon it might be, maybe in the near future, but not yet, not tonight."

I let out a breath and feel myself blushing.

"Listen, Mike, right now it's so complicated. Gooch is going to find out that I want my weight class back and he's not going to be happy."

"So you are going to wrestle him off?"

"As soon as you show me those moves you're always talking about." She kisses my cheek and heads up the aisle toward the front of the store.

Chapter 12

TWENTY-FOUR HOURS LATER, we meet in the aerobics room at Work-Out-World.

"Dude." She grins and holds out her fist.

I bump it with mine.

She drops her hoodie and strips off her sweats. She's looking fierce in guy's basketball Adidas shorts past her knees and a sleeveless spandex top with high-top wrestling shoes and a blue bandana tied backward around her head. We spread yoga mats, double thick, next to a warm-up mat.

"So, how did you get away from Gooch?"

"I come here all the time to work out. This is my gym." She smiles. "Also, Gooch doesn't have a membership."

"So, what do you want to learn?" I ask with a half-smile.

"You're the great Florida Mike," she smirks.

"Show me your stance."

She bends at the waist and watches herself in the mirrored wall.

"Hands higher," I say.

I push her left shoulder, then her right. Each time, she recovers her balance and assumes her stance. "Raise your chin," I say. "Keep your chest over your knees." I correct her feet from a square to a staggered stance. "Keep one foot in front of the other," I say. "Staggered."

We work on single-leg takedowns until she's moaning. I tell her she's still not fast enough, still not committing. When we tie up, I don't let her move in until she executes a head push. I try to concentrate completely on the wrestling, which is not happening. She smells something like cinnamon-cookie dough. Every time my face crosses hers I think about kissing her. The only thing that saves me is she's all about learning and getting better. She doesn't stop tugging and struggling, not for a second.

"Harder with a snap," I say. "It's supposed to divert a wrestler's attention. Push like you want to slam my head into the mat."

Face burning with frustration, she shoves the back of my head. When I push up, she rockets in for the high-upper leg. "Now drive with your head high," I say. "Lift and dump me."

She is a quick learner, but still holding back. Why? Is she scared to commit to a move? Scared she's not going to be able to finish it? Afraid she'll get hurt?

The next evening, she arrives at Work-Out-World looking worn out. Coach Rankin's practices are taking their toll. She heaves a breath and says, "Let's do this."

I stay on the basics - stance, control, single and double-leg takedowns. I show her a new version of an ankle pick and what to do with the leg once you have it in your grasp. We practice riding techniques, first her in bottom referee's position under me, then with me over her. I relax and admire her speed, technique and flexibility. I don't know if she's strong or quick enough to put Gooch on JV, but she is pretty awesome. "You could use more upper body strength," I say.

"Like I don't know that?" she says. "Why do you think I go to this gym?"

"I've got to be honest with you, right?"

"Whatever," she answers.

I wait for her on Wednesday night. By eight thirty, I've sent three messages. She finally texts back a sad emoji teddy bear with tears in its eyes and the message:

- *Things @ home are craz. I can't get there.*

- *what's goin down???*

Shelby: *Tell u later c u @ school*

But the next day, she's not in school. I'm sitting in our college writing class watching the door for her late arrival when Janice shoots me a text from her first row seat:

- *What are you doing this weekend?*

I text: *Wrestling, sleeping, working same ole same ole*

Janice: *Want to hang out?* ☺

I sit there for a minute staring at my phone and finally type:

- *can't still unpacking and stuff.*

Janice: *Cool cu at the match*

At lunch I pick at a can of tuna waiting for a message from Shelby.

I text:

- *r u sick?*

- is it your fam?

Nothing comes back.

At eight o'clock that night, she's in the aerobics room at W-O-W, sitting against the mirrored wall, holding her knees on her chest.

"You ever get tired of people who say one thing and do another?" she asks pulling off her sweats. Her pink t-shirt says, "*Yes - I'm a GIRL, Yes - I GRAPPLE.*"

"All the time," I say and think of my mother. She's been quitting cigarettes and vodka ever since I can remember.

"My father can be a first class bully," she says. "But you didn't hear that from me because he's the principal and you're not supposed to know that and I'm not supposed to say it."

"Don't worry," I say. "You can trust me." A long moment passes with her looking at the gym mat. Finally, I say, "My birth certificate came in the mail today."

"Which means I'm back on JV," she says. "Or I'm wrestling-off Gooch for 132. Which is it?"

"You tell me."

"Then give me something to shake him up. Even if I lose, I want him to know I'm not the same wrestler he remembers."

"So you're wrestling him?"

"Right now I am," she says. "Show me what you're going to use on Vladimir Roister," she says cockily. "Have you seen his videos on YouTube?"

I have seen them.

"I'm not telling you to worry," she says, "but I'm glad I'm not wrestling him."

115

"You're not helping my head right now," I say. "I don't want to think about losing, only about how to win."

"Right, because you don't know much about losing," she scoffs. "You've lost twice, right? Both times in a state tournament."

"You know what," I say. "Let's stop talking about winning and losing, and wrestle."

We tie up. She does a hard head snap and takes me down. I tumble backward. We get up and face off.

"Gooch won't be expecting a hip toss," I say.

"Then show me."

The move is violent, dramatic, a move not usually seen in high school wrestling. If it's not done with control, the ref could issue a penalty for roughness. I've used it in matches maybe a dozen times. "Once, you commit to the throw, you can't quit," I say.

I face off against her, explain the mechanics of the move, how strength comes from the wrestler's legs until momentum takes over. "It's all about believing you can do it," I say.

"I don't need the philosophy of wrestling," she says. "Show me the move."

I take it slow, very slow. Tell her to bend her knees and keep her hips low. I move her arms into an over-under-clench.

"Now start taking me off balance," I say. "Step to your right, spin and pivot." Her hip thumps into my gut. "Bend your knees into a squat and pull." My feet leave the mat. "Now spring up and throw me." She drags me over her hip.

I almost tumble on top of her. We are face to face, looking

into each other's eyes. I want to take her in my arms.

"I think you should get off me," she says, quietly.

We practice the move over and over until she's at full speed and flinging me to the mat. People gather at the aerobics' room window to watch. I teach her the Gazzoni, a move I learned at a tenth-grade wrestling camp. The Gazzoni is triggered when the bottom wrestler performs a "sit-out," and the top wrestler makes the mistake of reaching over the bottom wrestler's shoulder. Shelby catches on fast and really likes the move. We work until we are dripping with sweat.

"Break time," she says.

She sits crossed-legged on the mat, wipes her face with a towel and taps a text on her phone. Across from her, I rest back on my elbows.

"Why was your teddy bear crying?" I ask.

She pauses her thumbs and looks at me. "My parents. It's nothing new." She goes back to her phone.

"Is it serious?"

A flicker of pain crosses her face. "Not as serious as it could be."

"Are they fighting?"

She drops her phone into her backpack. "If I tell you, promise me, it's between us and only us?"

I promise.

"They argue all the time. They don't get physical or anything like that. They just say the meanest things to each other. My mother doesn't work and my father uses that against her. If she buys something for herself, he reminds her that he's the breadwinner. He's the one that sacrificed his body and all the money in the bank can't buy him back his knees. He's good at making her feel worthless. That's about the meanest thing you can do to a person. When she can't take it anymore, she goes after him, which is easy because deep down, I think he's completely insecure. That's why he's at the gym every morning at five thirty. He thinks he has to maintain his image as a NFL football player. And then there's his job."

"What about it?"

"Kinda complicated," she says. "He is the boss. A lot of teachers don't like anyone telling them what to do. And believe me, some of them, not all, resent him."

"Why?"

"Because they think he used his race and his NFL career to get his job."

I think of Janice's remark. *If she's what you're into....*

"So you stayed home because they were fighting?" I ask.

"No, I had bad cramps. I'm not on a regular cycle."

"Oh." I know my face must be turning red.

She exhales loudly and smacks my knee. "It's okay. It's not that unusual for female athletes." She fishes around in her backpack, finds a lip-gloss and removes the cap. I smell raspberry.

"Can I tell you what has been going around?" she says

"Sure."

"Some of the guys think you left Florida because you're in trouble with the police."

"Nah, nothing that exciting." I sigh and look at Shelby's perfectly smooth muscular thighs and her beat-up knees.

"Your father knows," I say. "It's in all in my file."

She shakes her head, "He would never tell me."

I sigh with relief. I don't want to be a subject at their dinner table.

"Tell me only if you want to," she says.

Despite myself, I start talking. "It started when my mother's boyfriend moved in," I say. "It was like one day it was my mom and me and the next, Mom, Jerry and me. He was okay like for about five minutes, then he started bossing me around, reminding me twenty thousand times a day to take out the garbage or cut the lawn."

"What about your mother?" asks Shelby. "Did she stick up for you?"

"She did and she didn't. My aunt says my mother makes bad life choices because she has low self-esteem. So anyway, Jerry took over the house. I couldn't be in it with him for five minutes without the shit hitting the fan. But it was more than Jerry. I had a fight at school. I hit this football jock, Kyle Scruggs. If I didn't leave school, I was going to be expelled."

"Hit him?" says Shelby. "What exactly does that mean?"

"It was a fight, sort of a long story."

"I'm a principal's daughter. I know you don't get expelled for one fight?"

"You're right, there were a few fights. So it was decided that I would live with my aunt and finish high school here. Sort of start over. Jerry and I weren't getting along and for everyone except me it seemed perfect."

"And your aunt?" asks Shelby. "What's she like?"

"She's not a phony," I say. "She tells me what she expects. She's good listener. Sometimes she acts goofy, telling me she believes in the power of a hug. Whatever that means. She cooks only healthy foods. Junk food isn't allowed in the house. She thinks a rice cake is a big treat, which is fine with me. She also keeps track of my calories. We started marking my height on the kitchen wall. She says the reason I'm so hungry is I'm having a growth spurt."

I start to push up from the floor.

Shelby takes my wrist. "Do you think I could beat Gooch?" she asks.

"You have to want it," I say.

Chapter 13

MATCH DAY, I'm pacing like a tiger in a cage, one side of the gym to the other, trying to keep Vladimir Roister out of my head. I have never let an opponent's reputation get under my skin, but today's match feels different, is different. The thought of losing now, losing in front of Shelby, is paralyzing. My eyes find her across the gym at the ref's table with Janice. Did I put her on the sidelines so that I could lose?

I tell myself to breathe.

In.

Out.

Relax.

Get loose.

The gym bursts with cheers as a Red Devil earns a reversal. So far, the matches have been pretty even. They win one. We take one. They pin. We pin. They take the lead. We take it back.

Gooch comes along side. "You checking out Vladimir? Did you know he's a cyborg, half-man, half-pinning machine?"

My eyes find Vladimir Roister on the Red Devils' sideline. He's standing at the end of line of folding chairs, staring at me with the intensity of a hawk.

His t-shirt says:

Eat-Sleep

Wrestle-Repeat

"You have any last words?" asks Gooch.

"When he loses, he can wash his car with that shirt," I say.

"Yeah, right," says Gooch. "Only one problem, he's not going to lose."

"He will today," I say.

Gooch laughs, "Keep dreaming."

With his words sitting like a fist in my gut, I say, "Let me help you warm up for your match."

He shrugs and follows me into a twenty-by-twenty foot room that's wall-to-wall wrestling mats. During basketball games in the main gym, the team uses the room for practice. "So you think I should be nervous?" I ask, shutting the door behind us.

"Well, he is-."

Gooch doesn't finish his sentence. I swoop in, grab his leg at the ankle and raise it fast. He falls to his stomach and I'm over him with an armbar across his face. I throw in legs and crank down on him. "So how about if you cut the shit," I whisper in his ear.

He grunts something.

"We're supposed to be teammates," I say. "You don't ask your teammate if he has any last words. You don't tell your teammate that he's going to lose. Do you understand?" I tighten my grip. "Do you?"

Gooch manages a, "Yes, okay."

"Because I want you to win and you need to want me to win.

You got that?"

"Yes, I got it."

I roll him and stick him on his back with my weight on his chest. "And if you ever pull your car away from me like you did or try any other bullshit stunts, I'm going to wrestle you hard everyday in practice. You got that?"

"Okay, it's cool, we're cool," he says.

Shelby and Janice give the mat a quick cleaning before Gooch's match. One swings a mop, the other sprays a mist of watered-down bleach. Shelby's dad watches from the gym doors where he always stands. I'm sure he's smoldering. His daughter went from varsity wrestler to the clean-up crew.

"Hey," says Dustin. "Looks like it could be up to you to save us from defeat."

The scoreboard reads: Red Devils 32 – Minutemen 34.

Dustin is right. I'm up last in the rotation, making me the finisher.

I start my pre-match routine, pacing and pullups. Today, I'm really hyped. *Okay,* I say in my head. *Big moves. A big win. Show them who you are. No fear. No doubts. Be quick. Be strong. Be focused. Think wrestling.* I breathe deeply and will my muscles to relax. "Wrestle my match, not his," I whisper. "Wrestle to win. Wrestle to pin."

I clap and release a long breath.

Gooch's match has started. Our side of the gym begins rhythmic pounding of feet on wooden bleachers, loud as claps of thunder.

Boom, boom, clap.

Boom, boom, clap.

Gooch is immediately taken down. He scrambles to his feet, goes in for a shot, but stays too high. His opponent collar ties him around the neck, and sets up for a screw-lock throw. Gooch is caught. A moment later, he's thrown to his back. The referee goes flat on his stomach and the gym goes nuts. Everyone yelling for Gooch to get up. He fights, twists, turns. The clock counts down the first period. He only needs to last another ten seconds.

Bam, pinned.

Over.

Devils fans shoot to their feet cheering and clapping. Their team moves ahead, 38 to 34.

I watch Gooch get up slow. Red-faced, nose bloodied, he shakes his opponent's hand and stumbles toward the Minutemen's line of folding chairs. My eyes go the corner of the mat where his dad stands solid as a stonewall. Mr. Goochinov's face wears no expression. With his arms folded tight on his chest, he rocks forward onto his toes and back, then up again. So many emotions pound through me. Gooch is so lucky to have his dad here, but how much does it hurt to lose in front of your father when he wants it so bad for you? I can't even imagine it. Gooch slips into a team chair and hangs his head between his knees.

Shelby takes the seat next to him, rubs his shoulder and says something in his ear. Gooch doesn't move.

The loss means my match determines the match winner. I

lose, the Minutemen lose.

Coach Rankin peers into my face. "You ready? You feeling alright?"

"I'm good."

"Don't leave anything out there. Understood?"

I nod.

The away crowd chants – "Vlad-di-meer, Vlad-di-meer."

Someone from the away side shouts, "Too bad you're gonna lose, Florida."

I enter the mat's inner circle, secure my headgear and place my right toe on the starting line.

Vladimir Roister, his body chiseled to muscle and bone, impossibly large for 138-pounds, works his lips over his mouthpiece, taps his fingers to his toes and leaps into the air.

Sweat breaks on my forehead. I glance into the throng of spectators and do a double take. Aunt Maggie and Tony from W-O-W are waving from the bleachers.

The ref says, "Keep it clean. Wrestle on my whistle and listen for commands."

I nod and shake Vladimir's hand.

At the whistle, we lock up. I expected his strength, but still I'm stunned by it. I struggle to stay on my toes. We separate and circle.

Vladimir's open hand smacks my forehead. He does it again, this time harder.

I glance at the ref, hoping Vladimir is given a warning.

Vladimir shoots for a single-leg. I sprawl hard on his back and spin behind him trying for a two-point takedown. He has my arm and we fight for position, roll, and fight again. He is not giving points easily and I didn't except him too. I rip away from his grasp and bingo, I'm behind him. The ref signals two points.

Before I gain further control, he breaks free and is on his feet, earning one point for the escape.

We circle. He smacks my head and shoots. His arms stay high and wrap my waist for a perfect duck-under.

Thrown to my butt, I work my arms around the back of his neck. We stay locked like this for a good twenty seconds. I listen to his breath near my ear until the ref sounds his whistle declaring a stalemate.

I'm still ahead, two to one and wonder how to handle his strength.

We set up again with our feet in neutral position. At the whistle, he attacks and tosses me off balance.

Finally, period one ends.

Pounding feet, hoots and the chant, "Vla-di-meer, Vla-di-meer!" echoes from the away side of the gym.

I look to Coach Rankin.

"Relax, steady pressure," he shouts. "You have this!"

Vladimir chooses bottom defensive position. I kneel and think, try a near-side cradle. The number one pinning move. Do it. Wait for the opening. Look for it.

Vladimir's right leg springs forward. Anticipating the move, I reach into the cradle, right arm around Vladimir's neck, left arm under his knee. I secure my hands using a standard butterfly lock and drive forward with a three quarter turn. Vladimir rotates onto his back and, like a roped steer, he's caught. One leg and his head are inside my cradle. He struggles, kicking and bucking his body. On my toes, I pull the Red Devil in and roll him onto his hip. I've been told I have an unbelievable grip and I'm locked in.

With Vladimir's legs kicking in the air, his butt pointing to the rafters, I earn back points and maneuver his shoulders trying to hold them to the mat.

The ref moves in closer.

Spectators rise to their feet.

Gym noise disintegrates into a cacophony of hushed voices.

I tighten the cradle. Vladimir's body folds in half. His face is buried in his chest. His fingers rip at my hands. I must hold on and keep my grip. I rock his shoulders to the mat and the whistle sounds. I wonder if I won or is period two over? Rankin is clapping and the gym is a wall of shouts and applause.

I won? I pinned?

I spring to my feet and throw my arms in the air.

The scoreboard flips - Red Devils 38, Minutemen 40.

My teammates swarm the mat, high fiving and hugging. Shelby is laughing at my side. I'm smiling so hard, I have tears in my eyes. Everyone is yelling, "Nice move," into my ear.

After the meet, Shelby and the girls crash the boy's locker room. This sort of blows my mind, because some of the guys were getting undressed. Mookie blasts a rap. Shelby grabs someone's antiperspirant, holds it to her mouth like a microphone and lip-syncs. Even Janice hams it up while the guys stomp their feet and bang the lockers.

Coach Rankin comes in. Everyone freezes. Playing the moment, he flips his hat backward and does this really goofy dance, then gets serious and yells for the girls to, "Beat it, now!"

I sit and soak in the victory. I'm feeling part of something good, part of a real team. I know from my other teams, winning does this.

Coach Rankin takes the antiperspirant can from Mookie and imitates a rapper, striding around hunched over, mouthing into the make-believe mike. Then he dances a herky-jerky robot so incredibly terrible, I'm laughing until my eyes tear.

Someone taps my shoulder. I turn and peer into Principal Hoffman's face. He isn't laughing or smiling.

"Mike, could I have a word with you?"

Throat dry, I follow him from the locker room into the gym. A word? What does that mean?

The mats are being rolled by the freshman team for the afternoon's basketball game. A janitor works a dust mop across the court.

"Sorry to take you away from that," he says.

I swallow.

"You wrestled tough and made it look easy. That move you used, does it have a name?" The Principal's eyes crinkle at the corners.

"Near-side cradle. It's pretty common. I used it a lot in Daytona."

A wide smile breaks on his face. "I didn't see it coming."

I nod wondering if it's ever a good thing to have the principal's attention.

"Well, here's what I'm thinking," he says. "Shelby's been keeping me up to date with her progress. I don't know if she's told you but she's shown me a few of the moves." He laughs and I see he's blushing. "So, do you think she'll be ready for her wrestle-off?"

"You mean with Gooch?"

"Exactly."

I tell him I don't want to answer for Shelby.

Principal Hoffman's shoulders bunch up. "She may not have told you but that's the whole point of her lessons with you."

Lessons? Is that what Shelby calls our meetings at the gym?

"Believe me," he says, "she wants a spot on varsity and you're completely right, in order to win she has to wrestle at her weight class. Mike, I want you to understand that I had no problem with your wrestle-off. You beat her fair and square. At 138, her season would have been all uphill."

"Yeah, it would have," I agree.

"But she wants it bad," he says, jumping in. "And that makes all the difference. She owes it to herself."

Janice and Shelby come laughing out of the girl's locker room. Seeing her father talking to me, drops Shelby's smile and freezes her in her tracks.

Principal Hoffman gives my shoulder a quick rub. "We can talk tonight. You're coming for dinner, isn't that right?"

"You mean today, tonight?"

He looks at Shelby then back at me. "Shelby didn't tell you? We're celebrating the team's win."

Chapter 14

AFTER THE MATCH, I clean the locker room at Work-Out-World, then hit the weight room for super-sets of chest and legs. I move fast with no breaks between exercises. I've been getting into a good routine and having the gym job is paying off. When I finally arrive at my aunt's house, she's waiting for me with her coat on and her pocketbook over her shoulder. The rest of the afternoon is a blur of rushing to the mall with Aunt Maggie. "You're not showing up at the principal's door looking like a rag-a-muffin," she says.

I try on pants and shirts and step from dressing rooms like a ten-year-old.

"Not that pair," she quips. "Too loose." She sticks her fingers into the waistline and tugs. "How do they feel? I think the crotch is too baggy."

Also stressing me out, Janice has been blowing up my phone with texts:

- *Movies tonight?*

- *Do you like sci fi???*

Each text makes me more anxious. Do I tell her I'm eating at Shelby's house? Why didn't Shelby tell her? Won't she find out? Should I even care?

My response is no response.

In Macy's, while my aunt flips through a stack of V-neck sweaters, Janice texts me selfies. I suppose they're supposed to be glamour shots, but her exaggerated pout reminds me of a duck's face. I need to text her back. I hate it when people ignore my messages.

I text:

- *U should b a model*

Janice: *You really think??*

- *Yes*

Janice: ☺

My aunt, the expert shopper, lugs armfuls of new clothes and a pair of shoes to various registers. She pays with a credit card and gives me a wink. "You're going to look so sporty tonight," she says.

Sporty?

On the ride home, her phone buzzes. The bluetooth activates and my mother's voice fills the car. "Can you talk?" she asks.

"Annie, Mike's here with me in the car. We were shopping," she says proudly. "I think we did pretty good, didn't we?"

"Yeah, Aunt Maggie bought me a bunch of stuff," I say.

"Jerry left me," she says. "He's gone."

"Permanently?" asks Aunt Maggie.

"How would I know?" she says with her voice rising. "We had a terrible fight."

"Did he hurt you?" I ask.

My mother catches her breath. "Remember those little crystal animals on the shelf over the stove?"

Her collection - a unicorn with a blue horn, a frog, a delicate fawn.

"In a million pieces," she says.

"But did he hurt *you*?" I ask.

"No, I'm okay. Listen Mike, you don't have to stay in New Jersey anymore," she says. "You can come home."

The first thing that smashes through my brain is, I don't want to leave. I don't want to go anywhere.

Aunt Maggie's knuckles are white on the steering wheel. "I don't think you're being fair to your son or me," she says. "We're getting settled and he's buckling down at school."

My mother almost shrieks, "Suppose Jerry doesn't come back. How do I pay the bills?"

"That has nothing to do with your son."

"Did Mike tell you I haven't been working?"

"Then find another job," says Aunt Maggie.

My mother laughs. "Great idea. I didn't think of that."

Aunt Maggie turns onto her block. She passes the now familiar ranch houses. "Annie, listen to me," she almost shouts. "Your son is about to have dinner with the principal's daughter and her family. I will call you back tonight and we'll figure this out."

"The principal's daughter?" asks my mom.

"Yes, the principal, and Mike has to get cleaned up and dressed." We pull into my aunt's driveway. She slams the gear lever into park.

My mother says, "Maggie, promise me you'll call."

With dusk closing, my aunt slows her car on a tree-lined street. The GPS tells us we've arrived at our location. A white brick mini-mansion with sculpted bushes and a large semicircular driveway is half hidden behind a stucco wall.

"Can you read the house number?" asks Aunt Maggie.

"That's got to be it," I say.

She pulls over.

"Be polite. Don't shovel your food and don't worry about your mother. I'll talk to her. You're not going back to Daytona, unless *you* want to go." She looks at me with watery eyes. "You look like such a gentleman," she says.

I grab the door handle and pause. "I have to ask you something?"

"Anything," she says.

"Why are you," I search for the right word. "I don't know, like, why are you so nice?"

"You mean to you?"

"Yes."

She turns her face to the windshield.

"I know you're my aunt and everything," I say. "But, I don't know if I can ever-."

She holds up her hand. "Repay me?"

"Yes."

"Mike, you don't owe me anything." She rests her hand on mine. "You and your mother are my only family. I thought I'd be the sister with a few kids, diapers and crazy holidays. It didn't happen. Life went on. I've been on my own a long time. So when your mother called, I looked at your stay with me like a gift, a chance to get to know my nephew." The corners of her mouth turn down and she reaches for my face. Holding my cheek, she places a light kiss on my forehead.

I start up a slate walk in black chinos, a button-down from the Banana Republic and new black Air Jordan Retro high tops. I brush the back of my pants checking for price tags. I'd feel more comfortable in my old clothes, but can't wait to see Shelby's face.

I'm carrying a bottle of sparkling cider from my aunt's pantry. She tied a bow around the neck of the bottle and curled the ends with a scissor. "You're not showing up on their doorstep empty handed," she said.

The door opens. Shelby crosses the porch and trots down the steps. "Tonight is already screwed," she says sharply. "My father is being an a-hole."

I practically freeze.

"Tonight is going to be all about me wrestling off Gooch," she says. "That's the only reason he invited you."

Do a full about face? Walk away? Call Aunt Maggie? She couldn't have gone far. I wet my lips. Inhale. Exhale. "Should I go?"

"It's just been a lot of yelling. Mostly by me." She tries a smile.

We sit on the wide steps attached to a broad porch that

connects to her house. Shelby looks more completely amazing than ever. She's wearing a cherry-pink denim skirt, a white button down top, sleeves rolled and maroon Doc Martens with red laces. Her strong legs jut from her skirt, one knee scabbed and mat-burned.

She says, "Do you know what I wish sometimes?"

I wait.

"I wish I was the girly-girl type, like Janice. A hundred and five pounds of spastic limbs, perfect hair and nails. All skinny and pretty, worrying about my makeup and lip-gloss. Then, maybe, my father wouldn't...." She sighs. "My dad's main problem is he doesn't know when to stop. That's what made him so good on the football field. He was the guy that believed he could win in the fourth quarter when the team was losing thirty-four nothing."

"Relentless," I say. "Like someone I know named, Shelby Hoffman."

"Is that a compliment?" She sort of smiles.

"I think so," I say.

"Thanks."

"You have a big house."

"Oh, you noticed." She glances at it over her shoulder. "My father calls it the house that football built."

I look at the way her calves fill her boots. So solid. "You look really nice."

"You don't think these boots are too much?" she asks.

"No, they're cool, sort of retro."

"If you want something safe to talk about during dinner,"

says Shelby, "ask my parents how they met. They like talking about that. It cheers them up."

"How did they meet?"

She smiles. "Ask and find out."

Chapter 15

THE FIRST THING I SEE, when I step into the Hoffman's foyer, is a full-size tree growing from a massive copper pot. The branches rise above a curved staircase.

"It's real," says Shelby, reading my mind. "Everyone asks that. My mother has a green thumb."

I follow her through the main hall. The air swims with delicious aromas of simmering beef, and somehow, there's this muted-classical music playing everywhere. I flash on my house in Daytona - the boom box on the refrigerator, the bottle of propane gas outside the kitchen window and the flex pipe snaked through the wall.

"Dad," calls Shelby. "Mike's here."

Almost instantly, Principal Hoffman hulks above me, square-faced as a superhero.

"Glad you could make it." He envelops my hand in his and gives it a concrete shake.

Shelby takes my bottle of cider and heads away. I want to go after her, but don't move.

"You follow football?" he asks, leading me into the living room.

"Sometimes, the Dolphins."

"I suppose you know what I did before settling here in Molly Pitcher."

I want to say, *Running back for the Saint Louis Rams*, but only one word comes out of my mouth, "Football."

"Not just football," he says. "The NFL. The difference is, anyone can play football, not many play in the NFL."

I take in the framed photos on the mantle. Shelby and her little brother line one side to the other. Principal Hoffman tells me to make myself comfortable. I sit across from him on a sofa.

He asks, "What do you think of my daughter?"

"Shelby?"

After a bellowing laugh, he says, "Is there another one?"

I'd like to say she's a beautiful person, but say, "She's a good athlete."

He laughs even harder. "Good one. Perfect. Best one yet. I ask that question to every boy she invites into this house. Do you know what one told me?"

"What?"

"That she didn't talk like a black girl." His laugh booms across the room.

A tall woman in tan skirt and a matching blouse comes in carrying drinks on a tray. What strikes me is Shelby's incredible resemblance to this woman, and the multitude of differences. For one, her mother is blonde, blue eyed and white. Her skin is lighter than mine. The principal is dark and bulky. Shelby's mother is the opposite, tall, light and slim.

"Are you telling that silly story?" she asks, setting the tray on the coffee table. "Did you mention that the boy was in the fifth grade?"

"Now you had to go and ruin my fun," says the principal.

"I'm Lynn Hoffman," she says. "I've heard a lot about you." She hands me a glass of cider. "And thank you for the thoughtful gift."

One thing for sure, my aunt was right about not showing up empty handed.

"Tell me," says Shelby's mom, "what brings you to New Jersey?"

"I already told her," says Shelby.

"It's called polite conversation," she says, and turns back to me.

"My mother wanted me to graduate from a good high school." I don't know where the lie comes from. "The school I was going to, it was pretty crazy."

"Crazy how?" she asks.

"Oh, you know, lots of fights. Kids smoking grass and cutting classes."

"I understand you're living with your aunt," she says. "I met her at Work-Out-World and take her Latin dance class."

"She's really into it," I say.

"I've noticed," she agrees.

The principal takes a gulp of cider. "Well, let's take this downstairs," he says. "And, somebody find Chad."

"Dad, I told you, I'm not doing this," says Shelby.

"It will take ten minutes," he says, eyes flashing on her.

139

"Show your father what you've learned," urges Shelby's mom. "It might be fun."

Shelby's mouth hardens. "This isn't fair. I'm wearing a skirt and Mike is dressed up. Mom, how would you like it if you had to wrestle right now?"

"Life isn't fair," says the principal. "Get your sweats on."

Beyond a mirrored bar and a humongous TV, beyond a leather couch, coffee table and a flashing juke box, beyond a row of exercise machines and walls coated with photos of football teams and a young Principal Hoffman in his uniform, about twelve feet of red wrestling mat covers the floor. A boy with curly hair, cut into a fade, stands on the mat. He's wearing a *Venom* t-shirt, chinos and yellow Nike running shoes.

"This is Chad," says Shelby. "My obnoxious brother."

"Now that's not nice," says Shelby's mom.

Chad ignores them. He flashes me a 'Rock-On' hand gesture - pointer finger and pinky sticking up, and says, "The notorious Florida Mike,"

"Chad is eleven going on twenty," says Shelby's mom.

He is absolutely big for an eleven-year-old. Almost as big as me.

"So here's what we're trying to accomplish," says Principal Hoffman. "Shelby has entered the women's county regional qualifiers."

Surprised, I turn to Shelby.

"I've never done a women's tournament," she says. "And my pushy father thinks I should wrestle some girls." She sticks out her tongue at her father.

He ignores her and turns to me. "She's also been working with Chad."

Chad, embarrassed, smiles.

"Mike, how about showing us a few of your moves?" says the principal. "Let's see what Shelby and you have been working on."

My eyes go to the mat. "Now?"

"I told him it was a dumb idea," says Shelby. "And I'm not changing into sweats."

"I'd like her to perfect the guillotine," says Principal Hoffman enthusiastically. "That's one move no one expects."

The moment is more than awkward. Shelby's mom tries to force her lips into a smile.

The principal smiles too broadly. "Oh, come on. You show us, then Shelby can practice it with her brother."

Still no one budges.

Chad gives this big nervous laugh like I'm getting punked and drops into referee's position on his hands and knees. "Come on, we do this, we can eat."

Unable to even glance at Shelby's face, I step on the mat, move in and over Chad and take top position.

"Walk me through it," says Principal Hoffman.

I clear my throat. "To hit the guillotine," I say, "the top wrestler has to control the bottom wrestler's hips." Hesitantly, I wrap my arm around Chad's thin waist.

Shelby lets out a loud moan. "This is so dumb. I already know the move."

"Then why haven't you used it?" snaps Principal Hoffman.

"Oh, like you've ever done a sport without a helmet," exclaims Shelby.

I grab Chad's left triceps. "Control the arm, then swing a leg in." I hook my leg under Chad's stomach, grab his far wrist and fall back on the mat.

Playing along, he rolls with me.

"Then I straighten out his arm and hook it behind my head." I work Chad's arm behind my head. "Next, lock the head." I complete the move by tightening my arms around Chad's head.

"Hey, take it easy," says Chad.

With Chad's arm extended, I press his shoulders to the mat. "It's a pinning move," I say.

"Nice." Principal Hoffman smiles. "Let's try it again, slower."

"Oh for goodness sake," scolds Shelby's mom. "Leave the boys alone."

Principal Hoffman barks, "Do you want her to win or lose?"

Shelby stomps up the stairs.

"Mike, show me," says the principal. "Once more."

The meal is pretty incredible; steaming string beans, mashed potatoes, peas and carrots, rolls, red cabbage and a football-sized eye round roast on a wooden carving board. Lavender candlelight flickers on the ceiling. At the head of the table,

Principal Hoffman carves the meat. Shelby's mom, at the other end of the table, looks over the food and her family with a pleased expression.

"Does Gooch know Florida is eating over," cracks Chad.

After a long moment of silence Shelby mutters, "His name is Mike and for once, can you not be a jerk."

"I bet Gooch doesn't know," giggles Chad.

"And he doesn't have to know," says the principal. "Because its none of his business."

"So don't tell him," warns Shelby.

Chad giggles and lets out a loud hiccup.

"Excuse yourself," says Shelby's mom. "Get a drink of water."

Chad pushes his chair out, lets out another hiccup. "I'll be back," he says in a deep voice trying to imitate the Terminator.

"He's at that age," says Shelby's mom. "We never know what's going to come out of his mouth."

Food is passed. I take a heaping spoonful from each dish. I don't even know if I like red cabbage. I've never tasted it.

"How's your mother?" asks Shelby's mom. "Do you stay in touch with her?"

"She's *his* mother," says Shelby. "Of course he stays in touch with her."

I chew a mouthful of string beans and swallow. "She's doing okay. Looking for work right now."

Chad returns holding a glass of water. He still has the hiccups. He smiles at me and sets the glass on the table.

"What line of work is she in?" asks Shelby's mom.

I wonder how to answer. Should I say a hostess or a waitress? Which sounds better?

"Why are you asking him this?" snaps Shelby.

Chad giggles.

The principal looks up from his plate. His eyes zero in on Chad.

"Shelby, I'd like to get to know Mike," says Shelby's mom.

"Really Mom? Is that what you call it? In my European history class it's called an inquisition."

Chad says, "They fight like this all the time."

Principal Hoffman leans over his plate. "Chad, knock off the shtick."

"How come I can't-."

He points his fork at Chad. "You're instigating and trying to be funny. And, you're not funny so I'm asking you politely to stop it. And Shelby, I didn't think your mother's question deserved your response."

"Let's drop it." Shelby's mom forces a smile.

"So what's living in a trailer park like?" asks Chad.

My spine goes straight. I could tell them that technically my house is not a trailer, it's a modular home, and my development is not a trailer park. It's a modular-home community. The houses are on real foundations, but I know it would make no difference to them.

Face crimson, Shelby's mom clangs her fork on her plate. "For goodness sake," she says. "Mike is our guest. Could we all be civil?"

"Mom, I saw you put his address in Google Earth," says Chad.

"I never," says Shelby's mom indignantly.

"You did so," says Chad. "You wanted to see if his house was in a nice area." He air quotes the words 'nice area.'

I put down my fork. I've Google-Earthed my house. My neighborhood is not a nice area. I picture the sneakers hanging on electric lines, the gully where everyone throws their garbage and the cars on jack stands.

"Mike, I apologize for my family's behavior," says Shelby's mom.

The principal clears his throat. "Let's enjoy the meal and change the subject."

"Boy these rolls are good," remarks Chad, wearing a grin.

Principal Hoffman points his finger at Chad. "Not another word out of you. I know what you're up to and we don't need your nonsense right now."

"Okay, sorry." Chad chews his roll.

"Not another word," warns the principal.

Shelby's fork trembles in her hand. She looks at me and tightens her mouth into a line.

"Just one more question?" says Chad looking at his father. "It's nothing bad. I swear." He crosses his heart with his fingers. "Mike, do you think Shelby can beat Gooch?"

"I will if I want to," says Shelby.

"Good," says Principal Hoffman. "That's the right attitude."

"But do you want to?" asks Chad.

"If I do win, I won't be doing it for anyone at this table," she answers.

"You might want to break up with Gooch first," says Chad.

"I don't have to because I'm not dating him," growls Shelby.

Her mom picks up her plate. "If you find another subject beside wrestling and this nonsense let me know." She heads into the kitchen.

I want to sprint for the door, then into the street under the trees, run until my chest hurts. Could everything I thought about Shelby's family be a lie? The big house, the NFL career, the Durango and Lexus in the driveway, the bloody pile of meat on the table, none of it is making anyone happy. Could living here be worse than living with Jerry?

"Lynn," calls the principal. "Come back and eat. The food is delicious and it's getting cold." He puts a large piece of meat in his mouth. Chewing, he turns to me. "What other moves have you taught Shelby? What's the one with the crazy name?"

"The Gazzoni," mutters Shelby.

"Gooch won't be expecting that," says the principal.

Chapter 16

MY AUNT KISSES my forehead during the ten o'clock news and goes off to bed. After 100 push-ups and fifteen minutes of crunches on my aunt's exercise ball, I curl up on the couch munching unsalted non-fat whole-wheat pretzels. With an afghan over my shoulders, I flick through television stations and settle for a movie about blood-sucking zombie-creatures taking over a cruise ship. On my laptop, I type in *Seaside Lions Wrestling*.

The site opens.

I find my next opponent's bio: Jake Longo – high school senior, lifetime record: 68 wins / 22 losses.

I Google Jake Longo and open an article from a local paper.

Longo PINS in Last Two Matches

Winning two matches in a row doesn't mean much. It's all about your opponents. I read to the end of the article and decide this guy shouldn't be a problem.

My mother's number flashes on my phone. Don't answer. Don't. Do I want to go back to Daytona? No, at least not now.

I answer. "Yeah."

"Mike? Is that you?" asks my mother, which is her usual greeting as if she calls my number and expects someone else.

"It's me," I say.

She laughs. Behind her voice, I hear the beat of music and voices.

"Where are you?" I ask.

"Believe it or not, I'm at Edith's Clam Hut out on Route 70. I used to come here with your father. That's how long it's been."

I've passed it many times on the way to the mall. Even stopped there with friends for fried fish sandwiches. I picture the oversize smiling clams and frowning crabs airbrushed on the walls. "What are you doing there?"

"Having a night out. I guess you could say, flying solo."

"You're drinking?" I ask, knowing the answer.

"Yes, but I'm watching it."

"Is Jerry still gone?"

"Michael, honey, I have my hand over my heart right now and I'm telling you, it's done, kaput. I shouldn't have let you leave."

I click off the TV.

"Here's what I've been wondering," she says as if it's our secret. "If I asked my sister for five hundred dollars, a loan of sorts, what do you think she'd say?"

"Aunt Maggie?"

She laughs. "I only have one sister."

I picture my mother at the bamboo bar hung with dusty straw hats, next to the slushy margarita mixer. "Mom, do you have the car?"

She laughs. "Do you think I walked ten miles to get here?"

"You should order a coffee and clear your head."

"I will."

"Promise me."

"I promise, now stop worrying. I'm a big girl." She laughs into the phone. "Does my sister make a good living?"

"I suppose. She puts in a lot of hours at the gym."

"So five hundred isn't too much, is it?"

"Why do you need the money?"

"I'm going to pay off my bills and get out of Florida."

"What about the house? I thought Jerry-."

She gives a choking laugh. "The taxes aren't the mortgage. The house is underwater. Do you know what that means?"

"Yes, but-."

"Then why are you asking about the house? That man at the bank, the one with the lemon-meringue rug on his head, he owns the house. You know what I own?"

I say what she has been saying since I was a kid. "The clothes on your back."

"That's right," she says.

My toes dig into the rug. "If you lose the house, where are you going to live?"

"Is there room for me there?"

"I don't know. You'd have to talk to your sister." I try to imagine the three of us watching television before bed, the three of us taking turns in the bathroom, my aunt lecturing my mother about her drinking and smoking. Is my new life about to careen off a cliff?

"Yes, that would be nice," she says. "A gin and tonic." My mother laughs. Then, the phone is picking up the bar's sounds - that song by Ed Sheeran starts, the one with the marimba mix.

A man's voice says, "Is anyone sitting here?"

Then, my mother is back with me. "Listen, honey, I gotta go." She laughs and disconnects.

Instantly furious, I call back and let it ring until her message picks up. "Mom, what was that? You call me and right in the middle of our conversation...." My anger is red hot and pulsing. I squeeze my eyes shut and toss the phone on the coffee table. Seconds later, it vibrates with a text.

Shelby: *my family is horrible right?*

- yer bro is a 1ˢᵗ class clown

Shelby: *I know and now my parents are fighting.*

- fighting bout wat

Shelby: *Probably me and it's loud*

- I forgot to ask how thy met

Shelby: *LOL*

- tell me

Shelby: *They were at an improve comedy club w their friends and they both got called up on stage. My father had to pretend to be a chicken and my mother was supposed to be the farmer's wife out to the barn to collect eggs.*

I'm smiling, trying to picture this.

- so yr ma had to do what??

Shelby: *Reach under my dad's butt and get imaginary eggs*

- lol

Shelby: *I know it is funny*

Chapter 17

THE SCHOOL DAY cruises by without a single extraordinary thing happening, at least until last period. Shelby clunks into class late wearing her Doc Martins, stretch jeans and a long sleeve Alicia Keys concert t-shirt that's pretty cool. I want to ask her about the shirt, but she chooses a desk on the other side of the room.

I text: *wat up?*

Shelby: *I'm doing it*

- *??*

Shelby: *wrestling off Gooch*

- *when???*

Shelby: *Today because I'm not sitting this season out*

- *Rankin nos?*

Shelby: *My dad told him but it was my decision*

After class, I follow her into the crowded hallway. She stops at her locker, works the combo lock, right, left, right. Opens it.

Before I say a word, she blurts, "Don't even ask if my father is making me do this. He's not."

"I wasn't going to."

"Good, because he's not."

Inside her locker door my eyes stop on a photo of her and Gooch at the junior prom. Shelby's rockin' a mini-princess dress. Gooch wears a tux with tails. Showboating, of course. She follows my gaze to the picture.

Her face flushes. "That was last year," she says slamming her locker door closed.

Our eyes meet.

I murmur, "Does Gooch know you're challenging him?"

"No, but he found out you were at my house last night for dinner. I forgot to swear Janice to secrecy. Like she doesn't know better."

"So Gooch knows. Is that a problem?"

"Look Mike, this isn't about you or Gooch. It's about me. I want to have a varsity season. I have to at least try." She pushes past, then stops. "And you know what? If I were a guy, you wouldn't expect anything else. It would be automatic, wouldn't it? Best wrestler wrestles, isn't that the way you took my weight class."

Shelby steps from the locker room - red singlet, white high-top wrestling shoes laced and tied, two large kneepads on her shins, hair tucked in a net, her makeup-less face icy calm. She slips on her headgear and snaps the chinstrap in place. Wrestlers usually don't wear singlets for wrestle-offs, but Shelby told me it's different for girls. "Tight singlets are good protection," she said, then added, "And don't ask from what. I'm not going there."

I swing my eyes to Gooch. He's goofing around, play wrestling Mookie. Could he know what's about to happen? Could he be that confident? I suppose he could.

Rankin leaves his office, strides to the center of the mat, waves his arms and calls, "Bring it in."

Wrestlers jog over and take a knee. Shelby stands behind the wrestlers with her arms crossed.

"We have a wrestle-off at 132," announces Rankin.

LaRocca says, "What? That's Gooch."

Eyes flash to Gooch, then to Shelby.

"Coach, come off it," announces Gooch, pointing at Shelby. "This is a waste of time. She can't beat me." He looks around for support.

Coach Rankin cuts through the team and places his arm on Gooch's shoulders. He walks him to the side of the gym. Gooch listens for about ten seconds with his eyes on the gym floor, then breaks away from the coach.

"Like I care," he shouts to everyone. He pulls off his t-shirt and throws it into the bleachers. Shirtless, he's not ripped. The elastic on his shorts presses into his stomach and around his hips. "She wants to get schooled, that's fine with me!" He storms into the locker room.

A hush falls over the team; everyone holding their breaths, everyone frozen in place, except Shelby. She's bouncing easily from one foot to the other. Her eyes vacant.

I feel like I'm standing at the end of a diving board looking into an empty cement pool. I don't see this ending well for Shelby. Rankin didn't make Gooch weigh in. He could be pushing 135. He could use that advantage and muscle Shelby to the mat.

A minute later, Gooch stomps onto the mat, eyes wired, motions jerky, like he had been caged for a long time and broken free. He's wearing shorts, a t-shirt and his wrestling shoes. He does a boxer's shuffle-step dance. "Let's go," he shouts in a voice tight with outrage. "I'm ready."

"Teach her a lesson she won't forget," mutters LaRocca.

I turn quickly to him.

"Don't look at me like that," he says. "We all know she sucks."

My nerve ends are twitching. I feel a rush of adrenalin and picture my fist busting his ugly mug. The big goon would never know what hit him.

Shelby strides onto the mat and stops three feet from Gooch. At first glance, she looks strong, sleek and solid, but, next to Gooch, she's all around smaller. He's taller and wider across his chest and shoulders. His arms are muscled. Only Shelby's legs are more muscular, her hips broader. She does look tough to take down, but anyone with eyes would bet on Gooch.

LaRocca cups his mouth and shouts, "Battle of the sexes."

The guys crack up.

"Gooch, don't fall in love out there," someone bellows.

Coach Rankin barks, "Next person to open their mouth is giving me laps." He steps between Gooch and Shelby and tells them to listen for the whistle and keep it clean.

Gooch clowns it up, smiling at the guys sprawled around the mat. He bows and pantomimes tipping a hat. He makes a pistol with his thumb and index finger, points at Shelby, lowers the trigger then blows imaginary smoke.

Mookie yells, "Barbie's mad at her Ken doll."

Everyone bursts out laughing.

"I said that's enough," snaps Coach Rankin. "Now, get running Mookie and don't stop until I tell you."

Mookie is about to protest, but sees the coach's face. His smile fades and he starts a slow jog around the gym.

A crack of light spears across the mats. Principal Hoffman, wearing a double-breasted suit, takes two steps into the gym and folds his arms.

Someone cracks, "Okay, now it's for real."

Shelby's eyes flick to her father, then back to Gooch. My heart halts, then resumes.

Gooch shrugs. "Let him watch his daughter lose. I don't care. This wasn't my idea."

Coach Rankin backs up, puts his whistle in his lips and blows.

Gooch attacks and locks arms with Shelby. His face is a contorted knurl of fury. They vie for inside position, hands grabbing and pushing off, more like a street fight than a wrestling match. Shelby goes for a collar tie. Gooch steps out of it, grabs her wrist and tries to fling her to the mat.

Gooch takes a clean shot and has Shelby's leg at the knee.

"Shelby, counter," I shout. "Counter."

She tumbles over and looks paralyzed. She can't give up now. I scream, "Head lock, head lock!"

She fastens her arm over Gooch's head, preventing him from gaining control and earning a takedown. They stay locked for twenty seconds with everyone yelling. Coach Rankin whistles for a stalemate.

First period ends with no score. Gooch isn't stomping around the mat with his chest out. He looks shaken and must know showboating is over. Shelby is for real.

Guys sprawl around the mat all eyes on the wrestlers. I stand at the edge of the circle. Shelby removes her mouthpiece and looks my way. "Where's my opening?" she mouths.

Every wrestler, including Gooch waits for my answer.

"He's wired," I shout. "Let him shoot. You counter." I want to say more, want to say, *Let him make mistakes and make him own them,* but she has already hustled to the center of the mat.

Second period and the brawl continues with more shoving, tying up and pushing off. Gooch manages an escape and goes up one to nothing.

Shelby waits for Gooch's attack, but he doesn't move in on her. It's like they're both in counter mode. Gooch, frustrated, raises his hands and looks to Coach Rankin wanting him to call Shelby for stalling. That's when Shelby goes in for a high crotch. Her head zips in under Gooch's outstretched left arm and her hip jams his midsection. Gooch tries to circle away, but Shelby is deep in the move.

"Holy crap," I say to no one.

Shelby pivots hard, grunts, swings her hips and launches Gooch air-born, head over heels. His wrestling shoes whack the mat, then he lands flat on his back. Shelby, over him, has his head and right shoulder tight in an arm lock. Gooch struggles, kicks. His strength bucks her into the air. She holds tight.

The team is on their feet. Everyone yelling.

Principal Hoffman's deep voice bellows, "Hold on. Shelby hold on."

LaRocca is screaming, "Bridge, Gooch bridge."

Seconds on the clock tick away.

Gooch goes to full bridge. The top of his head, his palms and his toes are the only part of him touching the mat. He rocks side to side.

Rankin blows his whistle.

Period two is over.

Shelby has earned two points for the takedown and three points for putting Gooch on his back. She leads 5 - 1.

The gym is a church and her father is a statue, eyes trained on his daughter. No one says a word. Guys exchange glances.

Third period, Gooch chooses down position.

Shelby glances my way.

I mouth, "Near-side cradle."

At the whistle, she has no chance at the cradle. Gooch explodes from under her grasp. He earns one point for the escape.

He circles, takes a hard diving shot and dumps Shelby on her butt. She scrambles and turns to her stomach. Gooch gets behind her for the takedown and earns two points.

Shelby - 5. Gooch - 4.

Shelby sits out and gets caught in the middle of the turn. She manages to hold onto Gooch's back. They go into a roll and tumble across the mat. Somehow, she winds up with an armlock around his head and arm. If she swings her foot between Gooch's legs, she'll have the guillotine.

I shout, "Plant your foot."

She maneuvers her leg between his and she rolls over, taking Gooch with her. He's on his back, one arm locked under Shelby's body. The other arm leveraged in her grip.

But she can't hold on. Gooch powers over Shelby and escapes in the scramble.

Rankin raises three fingers for Shelby's earned back points, two for the reversal and one finger for Gooch's escape.

Shelby - 10. Gooch - 5.

A minute left.

Exhausted, dripping sweat, they circle.

"Use the clock," I cry.

Each time Gooch comes at her to tie up, Shelby dances away.

My eyes slide from the clock to the mat, clock to the mat. Forty seconds left, an eternity on the mat. Gooch charges her.

Shelby pushes off.

Gooch lurches for her legs. She sprawls. He's under her and driving forward.

Twenty-five seconds left.

Gooch snags her ankle, works it into his body and scoots over, then behind her for two points. He throws in legs and flattens her to her stomach. Her headgear slips across her face. The straps are cutting into her throat. Gooch doesn't let up. Machine like, he slips his arm under her shoulder and clamps his hand on the back of her neck for a textbook half nelson.

He throws his entire body into the move. She fights it off, every muscle straining.

Gooch is on her, over her, trying to turn her. Their twisted faces inches apart. He's rocking her, side to side on the mat.

The principal yells, "Fight it. Fight it!"

A sick hole opens in my gut. If Shelby goes over, she could be pinned.

Five seconds.

Four.

Three.

Two.

One.

Coach Rankin sounds his whistle.

Shelby wins - 10 to 7.

The team holds their breath. Wide eyes stay locked on the wrestlers.

Gooch rips off his headgear. "Florida was telling her moves!" he yells and stomps across the mat. "Admit it," he says in my face. "You were coaching her."

"And you lost," I say. "Too bad."

Gooch steps back from me and turns to the team. His eyes are welling up. He shouts, "This is total bullshit!"

Everyone is watching him. I'm wondering if he's going to cry. The coach grabs him by the shoulders, turns him around and steers him into the locker room. I look for the principal. He's left the gym. Shelby goes to the bleachers, takes a long drink of Gatorade, wipes her wrist across her lips and smiles at me.

Chapter 18

BEFORE CLASSES, we meet near the gym doors in a shaft of early morning sun that sneaks over the tree line at the end of the football fields. Shelby reminds me of an urban warrior in her short leather jacket over a hoodie and faded blue jeans with both knees blown out. Her brown hair mixed with highlights, flows past her shoulders. In the light, it shines golden as honey.

She opens a paper bag and hands me a Starbucks in a white paper cup with a plastic lid. "My father bought them," she says. "He was in a good mood for a change."

The first bus rumbles along the looping drive toward the school. I take the coffee and feel its warmth in my hand. I'm more than thankful to be here with her.

"I talked to Gooch last night." She pauses. "He's pissed. Says it was an ambush and completely unfair. Says he should have been warned about the wrestle-off so that he could get mentally ready. I think he's only pissed about losing to me, a girl, which makes me so pissed. Like losing to me is a such a disgusting disgrace."

"What did he say about me?"

"Nothing good. He said you attacked him in the wrestling room. Did you?"

"I wouldn't call it an attack," I say. "And, it was nothing he didn't ask for."

"He thinks you and I formed an alliance against him." She smiles. "He wants a rematch. I told him anytime. And get this, he tells me I should consider quitting. Said all this junk about loyalty and friendship."

"Quit the team?" I say, hardly believing my ears.

"Yeah."

"Did you tell your father?"

"No, but can you believe last night he lectured me about my wrestle-off, said I should have pinned Gooch. I told him to stick to football."

I can't imagine anyone speaking to Principal Hoffman that way.

"Anyway," she says. "My goal right now is to win some matches, maybe have a winning season."

"Or be the first girl to win the Division," I say.

She smiles. "My father is expecting me to place in the women's county regional. First, second and third place finishers wrestle the North Jersey winners." She turns her face toward the murky sun and closes her eyes. "Can I ask you something?" she says. "Something sort of personal."

"Ask me anything."

"Did you have a lot of girlfriends in Florida?"

My laptop screen saver of Tara in a white bikini pops into my head. Could Shelby have seen it? "Not a lot," I say.

She draws an imaginary circle on the asphalt with the toe of her sneaker. "Some of the guys are saying you were like this player, that you had a ton of girlfriends."

"Who told you that?"

"It doesn't matter."

"Gooch?"

"Well, of course Gooch is one of them, but Mike, it really doesn't matter who said it or who thinks it. I'd like to know if it's true. Gooch's mother called me last night. She was complaining that you came into town and..." She doesn't finish her thought.

"And what?" I ask.

"And like screwed things up for Gooch."

I say, "You're the one who wrestled him off."

"I know, but that's what's going around and I don't want to be played."

I'm bewildered. It's my life that was tossed in a blender and turned on *Ice Crush*. I'm the one living with an aunt I'd only met a few times before moving in, the one who's getting calls from my drunken mother, the one considered trailer trash. Do I explain that in my entire life I've messed around with two girls; one from my block, the other Tara?

She asks, "Do you keep pictures of your girlfriends on your phone?"

"Why?"

"I'm interested."

I release an anxious breath between my teeth and pull my phone from my coat pocket.

She scrolls through my photos and stops at one of my mother sitting on Jerry's Harley.

"That's my mother."

"She's looks so young."

"She had me at seventeen."

Shelby swipes to a series of beach photos. Tara in a bikini. Tara on the boardwalk in flip-flops and shorty-shorts. "That's her, isn't it? Your girlfriend."

"My ex-girlfriend. When I moved here, we stopped talking and then we stopped texting. I think she already hooked up with someone."

"How tall is she?"

"Why does that matter?"

"She could be a model."

I take the phone back and begin deleting the photos.

"You don't have to do that."

"I want to."

"I hope you realize," she says. "I don't have to be here having coffee with you. I could be with Janice and the girls. I have choices."

"Then why are you here?"

"Why?" she says slowly. "Let me think." She gazes skyward. "I like your approach to life."

"What?" I almost laugh.

"You're like always thinking things through. And," she taps my nose, "you're this long-haired bad-ass jock on the outside, but somehow vulnerable on the inside. You also have old eyes. Did anyone ever tell you that?"

"All the time," I joke.

She swats at me. "You asked me a question. I'm trying to be serious."

I put my coffee down on the sidewalk and glance up the walkway. No one is coming. More than anything I want to kiss her. She must see it in my eyes.

"Don't' even think about," she says. "My father could be watching."

I look around.

"Right there." She points to the top of the building at a camera mounted on the front wall.

The bell for homeroom goes off like a gun. We both jump.

"Listen, I won't be in practice today," I say. "Rankin knows about it."

"You have to work?"

I don't want to tell her, but she's going to find out. "I'm getting braces."

"Braces on your teeth?"

I nod. "My aunt knows this doctor that does the procedure in one afternoon."

"An orthodontist?"

"Yes, she takes my aunt's aerobics class or something."

"You're kidding."

"You must have noticed I have the worst teeth."

"Not the worst," she says.

"My aunt set it up and offered to pay." Embarrassed, I finally exhale. "I know it's bad timing. I should wait until the season is over, but I've been waiting for braces since the sixth grade."

"How long will you have to wear them?"

I shrug.

"Well, good, go for it." She takes a gulp of coffee. "Come on, we'll be late."

Third period I have an *open study.* My options - sign into the library or sit in the computer lab at a workstation that doesn't connect to the Internet. I choose the library and find a table with a view of the outdoor basketball courts. I've been carrying around this beat-up paperback, *The Wanderers,* by Richard Price. The novel was stashed in my mother's room at the bottom of a drawer. I pull it from my backpack and spot Coach Rankin heading my way. He's wearing what he usually wears, a shirt and tie under a blue V-neck sweater.

"Do you have a minute to talk?"

I find my voice. "I guess."

"You guess?" he says.

I close the book. "I mean sure, of course."

He smiles. "You're not in trouble, so relax." He loosens his tie as if it's normal for us to be sitting across from each other. "I wanted to talk to you about Shelby."

I shift nervously.

"You worked with her after practice at the gym in town, correct?"

I nod.

"For how long?"

"I don't know, four or five times."

The coach's saggy eyes narrow. "How?"

"How?" I repeat.

"Yeah, how? How did you train her?"

"There's no rule against it, is there?" I ask.

"I'll tell you this, I didn't expect her to beat Gooch. She looked like a wrestler. Her win caught me like a left hook."

"She's tough," I say.

"I know she's tough. I just didn't think she could wrestle." He sighs. "Don't get me wrong, you did a good thing. It's just that I thought the team's starting line-up was set for the season." His face softens.

"So you think Shelby was lucky?" I ask.

"More like a fluke," says Rankin. "You know what a fluke is?"

"Yeah, you're saying it was sort of an accident."

"Roughly, yeah," he says. "So what did you show her?"

"First I taught her ten basic moves."

"What moves?" he asks.

"I could write them down." I get out my notebook and open it to a clean page. I number the lines on the page one through ten and print:

1. Double-leg takedown

2. Single-leg takedown

3. Sit out and turn

4. Half Nelson

5. Ankle Pick

6. Arm Cut

7. *Arm Drag*

8. *Cradle*

9. *Piute Roll*

10. *Sprawl*

I turn the book around. Rankin reads the list out loud.

"They're not in any order," I say.

"And why these moves?"

"My coach in Daytona kept these moves on a blackboard in the gym. He said it all starts with ten basic moves. After these moves, he taught us what he called the 'big boy moves.'"

Rankin slides the notebook back to me.

I print:

Gazzoni

Ball and Chain

Peterson

Butterfly

Cement Job

Barrel Roll

Spiral Ride

Guillotine

I slide the notebook back. Rankin rubs the stubble on his chin and looks over the moves.

"But it's more than just moves," I say. "I tried to teach Shelby not to be afraid of trying the moves. My coach in Daytona calls it 'Think Wrestling.' I don't know exactly how to explain that part of it. He said you have to wrestle with a plan in your head and visualize your win." I stare at the notebook for a moment, then at the coach.

"What else did he say?" asks Rankin.

"He said rolling around trying to survive, hoping to get lucky isn't wrestling. His favorite expression was, 'Think and execute,'"

Rankin, interested, asks for an example.

I take a moment. "Like if a wrestler is in referee's position, he should know his next move before the whistle. Always work toward a move."

"What if the move is blocked?"

"Then switch to another move," I answer.

Rankin counters, "What if the only thing to do is react to the other wrestler?"

"It's like flipping cards in your head," I say. "Even if you're in trouble, you go to the next move."

"And this works?" asks Rankin.

"It worked for most of the guys on our team." I shrug. "Some didn't get to the second level."

The coach shuts his tired eyes and opens them fast like he's had a sudden thought. "Okay, could you rip that page out of your notebook?"

Chapter 19

THE NEXT DAY I bite down hard on my custom mouth guard and jog around the gym wiping my lips on my sleeve, streaking it with blood. Every step shoots needles of pain into my lips. Yesterday, the orthodontist assured me that I'd get used to the braces, but it feels like she installed a Home Depot in my mouth. I tossed and turned half the night as the "painless" plastic and metal torture devices cut into my cheeks. Why didn't I wait until the end of the season? I asked the doctor if I'd be able to wrestle with them and she said they were *special braces.* "You won't be able to feel them."

Shelby slows and matches my stride. "You okay?"

"They hurt." I force a smile that's probably more like a grimace. "A lot."

"You picked blue for boys," she laughs. "Pretty rad."

"They ran out of purple polka dots."

"Mike, you'll survive. My eighth grade yearbook is about fifty pages of smiling construction sites and they all lived through it."

"Smiling construction sites? Is that supposed to make me feel better?"

"Sorry," she laughs. "That didn't come out right."

Dustin jogs up on my left. "Can I ask you something?" he says. "Isn't it kinda late for braces? I got my grills off when I was thirteen."

"Lucky you," I say.

"Wait till you get food stuck in them and all you do all day is try to get it out and your tongue gets sliced like bologna."

"Already happened," I say.

Dustin puckers his lips. "Wait until you're kissing your girlfriend and she's tasting yesterday's pepperoni pizza."

Shelby laughs. I try to laugh, but wonder if she'll ever want to kiss me.

"You hear about Gooch?" puffs Dustin. "His father took the keys to his Mustang."

"Then it's shoe-leather express for poor old Gooch," says Shelby.

Dustin cocks an eyebrow at me. "I also heard he might be out to kick some ass."

I laugh for the first time that day.

"He's a dirty fighter," says Dustin. "Last year at a party, I saw him hit a kid with a skateboard."

Rankin's whistle ends the run. Wrestlers lift their shirts, wipe sweat off their faces and head to the bleachers for their water bottles.

I try to imagine Gooch calling me out, a circle of guys egging us on. Gooch producing a chain or a baseball bat. That would be the only way he could ever win.

"Don't worry," hisses Shelby. "I know Gooch, he's not going to do anything."

The team forms a half circle around the coach. "We're going to try something a little different today," he announces. He crosses the gym and enters his office. A moment later, he rolls a white board on casters onto the mat. He's printed the ten basic moves in blue marker. "From this day forward," he says. "We are going to wrestle with a plan in our heads. Each of you is going to start with move one, perfect it, then go on to the next one. These are simple moves we should all know. It's nothing new."

Silence.

"Ok, lets line up and stretch'em out." Rankin blows his whistle.

Shelby smiles at me. "You told Rankin about the ten moves?"

Feeling a bit proud, my lips lift over my braces into a smile.

"This is awesome!" she says.

Wrestlers separate and form lines. Usually Gooch leads us through warm-ups. Today, no one takes his place.

"Shelby, take over," shouts Rankin. "You know the routine."

"Whoa, whoa, whoa," exclaims LaRocca, stepping out of line. "You expect us to listen to her? No way." He looks for support.

No one moves.

Shelby turns to the coach.

Rankin removes his glasses. Blinking and already agitated, he says, "Mr. Adam LaRocca, shut your face and get back in line."

LaRocca lets out a loud fake laugh. "Coach, no one is down with a her taking over our team. We don't want her leading us in anything."

"Get in line," barks Rankin. "Shelby, up here now and let's get started."

"Are you deaf?" says LaRocca, voice rising. "No one wants her here. She shouldn't even be on the team."

"Adam, go get dressed," orders Rankin. "You're done for today."

Face bright red, he stands his ground. "No, this is my team more than yours," he says.

At six foot one, two hundred pounds, LaRocca makes the coach look like what he is, a balding, slope-shouldered, old man with glasses.

"Today is over for you," says the coach. "Now get going before this becomes bigger than it already is."

LaRocca steps around the coach and peers down at Shelby. His eyes are rancid slits. "We don't want you here," he booms in her face. "No one ever did. Why don't you go with your own people!"

The hate in LaRocca's voice is icy cold and real.

"My people?" roars Shelby. "Who are my people? Say it, let me hear you say it!"

LaRocca tilts his head back and laughs, "Go look in a mirror."

I shove LaRocca in his chest, almost sending him off his feet. "Apologize."

He laughs. "You're telling me to apologize? This isn't your

team. This is my team. Gooch's and mine, and he's gonna be back. So don't go telling me what to do."

The air feels thick. The team is stuck in place like spectators at a car crash.

Rankin steps between us. He's on his phone, talking rapidly.

"Who are you calling?" shouts LaRocca. "Who?"

"The front office. Now get your ass out of my gym."

LaRocca doesn't move and I'm not backing down. We stay face to face.

Shelby tugs on my arm. "Please, Mike, don't."

I let her pull me away. If I hit LaRocca, I'll be back where I was in Daytona, out of school and off the team.

"It's over," whispers Shelby. "Don't fight him for me. He's not worth it."

LaRocca doesn't charge, doesn't raise his fists, just yells, "Look at Florida, pissing his pants."

I flinch and turn back to him.

"Don't," says Shelby. "Don't you dare do this for me."

Face sunburn red, LaRocca shouts, "This team is history."

For a moment, he waits for someone to come forward and take his side, but the team has backed away from him and seems stuck to the gym floor.

I call my aunt because the weather sucks and I don't want to be on the late bus. She picks me up from the front of the school and drives straight for home through a sleeting storm. The heat in the car is pumping, but I'm icy cold and sweaty, almost feverish. My mind rings with LaRocca's hateful words, *Why don't you go with your own people.* I don't know how Shelby stayed in control. So composed. After LaRocca left the gym, I was called out of practice to Principal Hoffman's office. I told him what happened and admitted that I'd shoved LaRocca.

"I'm not concerned about a shove in a wrestling room," said the principal.

He asked me to write a statement and sign it. Reading over my paper, rage creeping into his creased eyes, he asked, "And Adam LaRocca said these exact words?"

Embarrassed to have written it and embarrassed for him to read it, I nodded wondering why I didn't hit LaRocca. No one should get away with that.

Aunt Maggie drives slowly, eyes on the road. The only sounds are ice pelting the windshield and the scrape of crusted wipers. I realize she hasn't said a word to me, not even hello, and I'm wondering if someone from the school called her.

"What's the matter?" I ask.

"I have something to tell you." She slows and stops at a crosswalk. A little boy in a yellow slicker holds his mother's hand and they hurry across the street. "Your mother had an accident."

"With the car?"

"I don't have the facts yet. I do know she's been admitted to Daytona Hospital. I've been on the phone since two o'clock this afternoon."

"Hold on, what?" I didn't hear anything after the word, hospital.

She presses the gas. The rear tires slide, then grip the road.

"I don't know exactly what happened, at least not all of it. There are patient privacy regulations and your mother has to sign permission papers. The hospital would only tell me she's had her ankle reconstructed."

A tremble passes along my shoulders. Reconstructed?

Aunt Maggie turns onto an avenue of stately homes with wide old porches and brick stoops. I feel the sensation of the car tires slipping. Everything slipping.

"Did you tell them you're her sister?" I ask.

"Yes, of course. That's why they called me. At some point your mother listed me as an emergency contact. We'll know more soon. The hospital administrator is going to call me back."

"You're awfully calm," I say.

"No, I'm not. Believe me, I'm not. I'm in crisis mode."

The car skids onto Molly Pitcher Road. The main strip of the town has been recently salted. The road is black and wet. I feel like I'm in suspended animation, when I should be in shock. All I'm thinking is, *What now? What did she do now?*

We drive past the Judo studio, car lots, the pizza place and Chinese take-out. All deserted. Suddenly, a man dashes from the corner deli holding a pizza box over his head. My aunt wallops the brakes and cuts the wheels. The seatbelt tightens across my chest as the car slides to the shoulder of the road. We miss him by inches and he doesn't look back.

She bangs the heel of her palm on the steering wheel. "I could have killed him."

I wait for my heart to settle. "My mother would chase that

guy down and tell him off," I say.

"Your mother was the wild one," says Aunt Maggie, angrily. "Always a rebel. Like it's a badge of honor to have your parents get a five a.m. phone call letting them know their daughter was picked up drunk at the park."

"She did that?" I ask.

"And a lot worse."

At the house we make a run for the front door. Aunt Maggie works her key in the lock and shoves it open with her shoulder.

The house phone is ringing. She takes off down the hall.

"Hello, yes this is Margaret, her sister. Annie has a son and me, that's it," she says loudly into the phone. "Her husband passed on. Oh, I don't know, maybe fifteen years ago. No, she never remarried. Yes, I'm telling you there are no other blood relatives. Where do I live? Me?" Aunt Maggie stares wide eyed at me. "I live in New Jersey. No, I don't know if she applied for Medicaid." Her eyes stay on my face. She covers the phone with her palm. "Do you know if your mother has health insurance?"

"I guess," I say.

"You don't know?" Aunt Maggie rolls her eyes. "Did she give you an insurance card?"

I don't have to check my wallet. I shake my head and remember breaking my nose and my mother pulling the blood soaked cotton packing out of my nostrils to save a follow-up visit.

Answering questions, my aunt paces from the refrigerator to the stove. She finally hangs up.

"Your mother's had some kind of surgical procedure on her ankle. We are going to talk to her when she wakes from anesthesia."

I am cold all over. I suck in my lips against my braces and feel tingles of pain.

The doorbell rings.

I race to the window.

Shelby, still in her sweats, waits in the sleeting rain. The sight of her floods me with relief. I wipe my eyes on my sleeve and open the door.

"I stopped at Sultan Wok," she says and raises a white paper bag. "I thought we could have Chinese. It's lo-cal, all steamed."

I am immediately explaining that something happened to my mother. Shelby follows me to the kitchen and places the bag on the table.

The food smells delicious and I realize I'm starving.

"This must be Shelby Hoffman," says my aunt. "Mike's told me about you." My aunt holds the kettle under the running faucet. "Just another crazy day," she singsongs like every day is bedlam. "Mike's mother, my sister, has had an accident and some kind of operation on her ankle. She should be calling soon."

"I could go," says Shelby. "I thought Mike might need-."

Aunt Maggie's phone rings. She holds it so that I can see the screen and swipes the green FaceTime button.

My mother's face appears on the phone. Her head is propped on a pillow, hair tucked behind her ears. Even on the small screen, I notice her eyes are trashed.

"Are you there?" she asks groggily. "Can you see me? I can see you."

I take the phone from my aunt's hand. "Mom?"

"Mike, oh my God, it's so good to see your face and hear your voice." Tears leak from her eyes and drip down her cheeks.

"What happened?"

"I stepped off a curb," she manages to say. "I went one way and my foot went the other. The doctors put a rod in my ankle."

"A rod?"

She grimaces. "A titanium rod."

"Where, what curb?" I ask picturing my neighborhood, as there are no curbs on our street.

"I was out to lunch with friends," she says, wiping tears with her fingertips. "I went back to the clam hut on Route 70."

I picture the little restaurant and my mother stumbling out the front door. "For half-price margaritas, right?" I ask.

She hesitates, shuts her eyes. "I did have a margarita," she admits, "but I also ate lunch and it's not a crime to-."

"Was Jerry there?"

"No," she says. "I was with a few of my girlfriends."

My mother never had girlfriends. She had boyfriends.

"And you turned your ankle on the curb?" asks Aunt Maggie over my shoulder.

"Yes and now here I am."

I watch my mother's face. Something about the way her

eyebrows remain up, as if she's waiting for a challenge, tells me she's lying. I step away from the phone, look at Shelby and wish she wasn't seeing this. I want to shout, *My mother's lying. I know she's lying.*

My mother asks, "Did you get braces?"

Aunt Maggie takes over. "He's doing great with them," she says. "He's a real trooper."

"Mike, let me see. Give me a smile," says my mother.

I can't do it. "Forget it," I grunt.

"Oh, baby, come on," says my mother. "You know I was saving for them."

Another lie. Years ago, she labeled a five gallon water jug, *For Mike's Braces*, and began cramming dollar bills inside. The money was used for food, vodka, clothes, everything except braces.

"Maggie, I'm going to pay you back," she says. "You know I will."

"Don't be silly. It's a gift to my nephew. That's the way I want to keep it."

"No, no, come on now. I'll pay you back."

Again, an old familiar fury rises up my throat until I'm nearly choking. "How, Mom?" I blurt with my face inches from my phone. "How are you going to do that? You're in the hospital with no insurance."

Shelby places her hand on my elbow. "Mike, come on, she's had an accident."

Aunt Maggie turns the phone to her face. In a light voice she says, "Tell us about your ankle."

My mother starts with lunch. How she enjoyed her order of steamer clams dipped in butter. "You remember them, don't you Mike?" she asks.

"I never liked them," I say.

"I thought you did," she tries to laugh. "Well, anyway, after lunch I step into all that glare and the next thing I know, I'm on my back."

I want to say, *Ma, you forgot to mention your girlfriends.* Conveniently, left them out.

"I broke all three ankle bones," she says.

"Oh my god," whispers Shelby.

"Annie, do you have health insurance?" asks Aunt Maggie.

"No and I think the hospital wants to discharge me in the morning," she says. "I don't know what I'm going to do or how I'm going to manage?"

I don't want to do this in front of Shelby, but can't help myself. "Those friends at the restaurant with you," I say. "Who were they?" My words are rough and sound like someone else is speaking for me. "Name them."

"How does that have anything to-."

I cut her off. "It has everything to do with it." I grip the phone. "Everything!"

"Why do you want their names?" asks Shelby.

"Because I don't believe her," I say and feel the weight of Shelby's eyes.

My mother leans toward the camera on her phone. Her face is large and distorted. "If you're asking me if I was with Jerry," she spits. "Well, I was! I wanted to spare you that detail. Now you know and so what! It's not a crime." The screen goes gray and FaceTime ends.

Sometime after eleven that night, I'm in the kitchen eating a plate of leftover-microwaved Chinese when my aunt's bedroom door opens. Wearing men's pale blue pajamas, her face already numb from exhaustion, she holds her phone out to me.

"Your mom has something to tell you," she says.

I drop a soggy spear of broccoli onto my plate and take the phone.

"Honey?"

"What?" I say, voice hard as metal.

"Are you mad at me?"

"I don't know."

"Honey, I'm sorry."

Lightning flashes at the window and I hear rain hitting against the house.

"I didn't mean to lie to you," she says. "I think it was the pain killers."

"Mom, pain killers help you tell the truth." Thunder rumbles. I lift my eyes to my aunt. She's leaning with one hand against the refrigerator, watching me.

"Mike, honey," says my mother. "The truth is I was in a motorcycle accident. I don't know why I told you that stupid lie."

Her words bite into my flesh. Of course you were, I think. "Jerry's bike?"

"Yes, his Harley. He was going too fast like he always does,

183

but I can't blame him completely. I asked for a ride into town so that I could-."

"Stop!"

"Honey?"

"Stop. You're doing it again."

"Doing what?"

"Lying. You didn't need a ride into town. You went with him like you always do. Admit it."

"I swear to you. I needed a ride," she says desperately.

"For what?"

Seconds pass. "I had to get groceries."

Get groceries on a motorcycle? Yeah, right. She thinks I'm that little boy she shoved in his room when she had her boyfriends over. The little boy who could be told anything. The little boy who trusted her.

"Are you there?" she asks.

I push out a breath. "Yeah."

"We hit some gravel on that turn by East End and Coral Avenue where they have that old farm stand. Remember we used to stop there to buy fruit? Jerry couldn't control the bike. The back wheel went out."

I see the bike sliding, my mother's arms around Jerry's waist, the road coming up fast, sparks spraying hot blacktop.

"It happened so fast," she says. "I couldn't hold on. Jerry stayed on the bike, but I went flying through the air."

"Did he get hurt?"

"Oh, you know Jerry," she says like he's so remarkable, like he has a PHD in falling off motorcycles and not getting a scratch.

She goes on about her foot hitting the curb and shattering her ankle. "The ambulance took its sweet time getting there," she says. "I was sitting in the road and all the cars were stopped."

I press my lips into my braces, wince from the pain and whisper, "I wish you never met him."

"Now Mike, don't be-."

"Ma, he's not good for you." I hear the heat in my voice.

"He moved out," she says. "That's something, isn't it?"

A pressure starts in my temples. I shut my eyes. "What are you going to do now?"

"I could be covered under Jerry's motorcycle insurance policy." She offers a weak laugh. "So that's one good thing, right?"

"And you swear he's not living with you anymore?" Thunder booms and shakes the house.

"I'm not saying he's a stranger, but he's not living here. Not technically."

"What does that mean?"

"Sometimes if it's late he..."

I hold the phone out like it's a poisonous snake. My aunt takes it, puts it to her ear, listens then says, "Annie, of course he's going to be upset. You made up a story."

I go to my bedroom and shut the door.

Chapter 20

THREE DAYS LATER, I stuff old and new clothes into my backpack. I throw in my bathing suit, remove it, and then pack it. Yesterday, the trip felt doable and noble. I told myself that I was on a mission to help my mother. The plan was to get her stable and return to Jersey before Saturday's quad, when I'll face the undefeated Andrew Fox. My teachers agreed to email assignments. I'm not taking my textbooks and have no idea when I would have time for homework, but I smiled and thanked them. Coach Rankin put his arm on my shoulder and said, "Stop worrying. We'll all be here on Friday when you return."

Today, the journey home feels like a kick in my nuts. I should have told my mother, *No, absolutely not.* I should have waited until the end of the season. I don't like to miss practices, especially before a big match. But, there is one major problem, she is my mother. Even Shelby said, "Family comes first."

I've got that swimming feeling in my stomach, like any minute I could be sick. Why did I agree to go? Why? Leaving here now is a mistake. I'm sure of it. Dustin said no one expects me back and added, "Dude, Gooch is already talking about taking your weight class."

I squash everything into my backpack, zip it and check the time. Nine o'clock. Shelby's heading into Modern Chemistry. We said our goodbyes after yesterday's practice. I promised to be back soon. As I was walking away, she called my name. I followed her into an empty hall. She grabbed my t-shirt in her fist and pulled me close. It was our first kiss, and my first with braces. I felt like my feet left the floor, like the entire school disappeared. It would have to carry me through the trip.

I text her an emoji of a smiling monster holding a suitcase:

- *all packed leaving soon for airport*

I'd like to add - *missing u already.*

Shelby replies:

- *Take food last time I flew got nada*

- *thanks*

Shelby: *LaRocca was suspended a full week - pretty major.*

- *such an a-hole. Did he get kicked off the team?*

Shelby: *No just suspended but my dad says one more racial comment and he's done.*

Aunt Maggie set a big breakfast for me. Next to my scrambled eggs, whole-wheat toast and turkey bacon is my printed airline ticket.

Depart: Newark 12:05 pm

Arrive: Daytona 2:50 pm

I flip it over and read the small print. Turn it right side up, stare at it and ask, "Did you buy me a one-way ticket?"

Aunt Maggie turns from the stove. She's dressed for work in sneakers, tights and a long gray sweatshirt.

"How could I buy a round trip?" she says. "I don't know

when you're coming back."

My eyes return to the ticket. "I told you I have to be back by Friday night."

"I know, but we both know your mother."

"What's that supposed to mean?"

"She's a troubled person," says my aunt. "She might need your help for who knows how long. Can we leave it at that?"

"Oh, really," I say sarcastically. "A troubled person? Ya, think? Gee, thanks for filling me in, but I'm not blowing my season. I shouldn't have agreed to go in the first place."

"Now don't start second guessing yourself," she says. "You decided to go. She asked, you agreed." She comes to the table and points a spatula at me. "And, you better come back. Do you think I want to lose you now when we've been getting along so well? I don't. So go down there, help your mother. When you want to come back, I'll buy your ticket."

"What if she can't function by herself?"

Aunt Maggie frowns. The concern in her eyes deepens. "Ask her if she wants to come back with you. Tell her it's fine with me. We'll make room. If she doesn't want to come here, then you'll have to make a choice."

The Uber driver shows up exactly on time. I hustle to the door and shoulder my backpack. Aunt Maggie gives me a bone crushing hug and a kiss on my cheek. I don't say a word, can't. I'm holding everything tight inside my chest. I set off down the path and tell myself not to look back.

Chapter 21

FLORIDA IS OVERCAST, murky and hot. A warm breeze from the cab's open driver's window blows in my face. My neighborhood hasn't changed - squished-in houses, boats on lawns, dogs panting under trees, cars with flat tires, rusty pick-up trucks, patio umbrellas bungi-corded to fences. "Turn at the guy in the chair," I say.

The driver hangs a left at old man Jackson, asleep in his webbed chair next to his Igloo cooler. He slows and brakes at my house. The first thing I don't want to see is Jerry's Harley leaning on a stack of car tires. And, there it is on the front lawn with scrapes and gouges crisscrossing the gas tank. I remember the broken clutch pedal. He'll want his sixty dollars.

I pay the driver and add a two-dollar tip. He hardly looks at the money, just slams the gas and blows through the stop sign at the end of the block.

"I'm back here," calls my mother.

Jerry's empty beer bottles line the kitchen countertop, one side to the other. A soda can torn in half overflows with cigarettes butts. He has taken apart a carburetor at the table. Screwdrivers and small wrenches are scattered among gaskets and gray metal parts.

Her leg rests high on two pillows. Her toes stick from the end of a white cast like fat baby fingers. In the shadowed light, her face is the color of newspaper. She's wearing a camisole with one strap off her shoulder and a dozen gold chains and charms around her neck. She extends her arms. "Come here, come here." Her voice is choked and high. "Come over here."

Feeling wobbly, I move into the room. Her days in bed, the stale air and cigarettes swim up my nose.

Her arms wrap me. I hug her back. Some of my anxiety and regret lifts. No, I don't want to be here, but I tell myself a few days away are okay. I've missed practices before. I can run in the mornings and do pushups. And, she is my mother. It was always the two of us against Daytona, against Florida, against everything and everyone.

You aren't supposed to detect vodka on someone's breath, at least that's what my mother always told me, but I smell it. I look for the bottle with the ducks boxing, a label I thought was cool and tried to draw when I was a kid. The vodka rests on the floor next to a stack of tipped Cosmopolitan magazines. Same brand, same old label.

"Have you seen Jerry's new venture?" she asks.

"His bike?"

"No, take yourself a gander out the back window."

I open the blind. Outside, where there had once been a rusty laundry tree, my warped skateboard ramp and a picnic table, there's a square flat-roofed building with a rolling metal door and a rectangular window. Three yellow extension cords snake across the yard into the building.

"I told you Jerry was starting his own business," she says. "The building is all pre-fab. Only took three days."

"If you're done with him, what's that doing in our backyard?"

"It's for storage," she says. "Motorcycle parts and motors. Jerry is getting the word out. So far it's been slow, some welding, fixing flats and tune-ups, but it adds up."

A trickle of sweat runs my spine. "I thought you were losing the house to the bank?"

"My little worrier," she says in a voice mixed with happiness and affection. "Jerry's really been helping out. He's making payments, getting me caught up."

"Because he put a building in our yard?"

"Yes, and because he cares about me."

My insides feel twisted into tiny knots. "Mom, you told me you were through with him."

She cracks a smile. "We started over," she says. "We're putting all the bad behind us and having a lot of fun."

I tap her cast. "Fun?"

"Going down on the bike wasn't his fault. You know that turn. It's always in the paper with accidents."

It's like she believes her own lies. When is she going to wake up? "And you tell me this now?" I shout. "You couldn't have told me this yesterday. I'm missing school and wrestling."

"Don't be like that." She musses my hair. "I need you here. You and I went through a lot. We had our troubles, but, we're still here, right?"

"You made it sound like you and Jerry were finished."

"No I didn't," she exclaims.

"You did. If you don't believe me, call Aunt Maggie."

"I'm not allowed to have a boyfriend?" she says. "I'm not allowed to have a man in my life?"

Her familiar argument jabs like a sharp stick. She's the one who always has to have a life. I'm the one left standing by her side when it all goes wrong. "All I'm saying is you should have told me and you know it," my voice cracks with frustration. "If he cares about you so much, what am I doing here?"

"I missed you."

"I don't know," I say feeling helplessly trapped. "You always lie to me."

"You do realize I'm in serious pain and on medication. I'm going to need help around here."

I peer into her weary makeup-less face and ask if her ankle hurts.

"It did, but the doc gave me these." She clutches an amber pill bottle and shakes it like a baby's rattle.

"I saw Jerry's bike," I say.

"Yeah, developed a bad case of road rash."

"You're letting him rebuild his carburetor on our kitchen table?"

"You don't have to worry. Things are going to be so much better."

"How?"

"Well, to start with Jerry and I have come to an agreement. We're not drinking on the weekdays. Friday and Saturday nights we go out and have a good time."

"Oh, come off it," I say. "I can smell it on your breath."

"I had one sip for pain."

I shut my eyes and give up.

"Show me your braces."

I try a halfhearted smile.

"Baby blue for my baby boy."

"Mom, cut it out."

"You can hardly notice them," she says. "And I will pay my sister back."

The slam of a car door brings me to my feet.

"That could be Jerry," she says. "He's been checking on me."

Through the window, I catch sight of him in the yard. He looks the same: grease-stained painter jeans and a neon-yellow highway-worker's t-shirt from his days on a road crew. His straight brass-colored hair is pulled tight into a ponytail. He's lean and looks strong as rope. He works a key in the lock of his new shop, bends and lifts the door. Before he enters, he squints at the window and sets his jaw like a dog catching a scent in the air.

Chapter 22

MY MOTHER POINTS her cigarette at Jerry. "I told my son we gave up drinking on the weekdays."

"Annie, you gave it up," replies Jerry. "I said I'd cut down."

"That wasn't the deal," she chimes.

Jerry lifts his beer to his mouth, chugs and belches.

We are in the front yard, eating rotisserie chicken and biscuits off the tailgate of Jerry's F-150 pick-up, having what Jerry calls a "hillbilly picnic." The truck doors are open. ZZ Top is blasting. The early evening air is still hot, but the day's real heat has lost its strength. I help my mother into a webbed folding chair with aluminum arms and lift her casted ankle onto an overturned bucket.

Jerry crushes his beer can and stretches his tattooed arms along the bed of the truck. He's fresh from the shower, wet hair parted firmly in the middle. "Heard they almost dropped 'rastling from the Olympics," he says.

"But they didn't," says my mother.

I ignore him and shoot Shelby a text:

- *It sucks here*

Shelby: *send me a photo*

- *of what*

Shelby: *your mom*

- *nah shes messed up*

Shelby: *her ankle???*

- *that and a lot more - guess who is here w me*

Shelby: *??*

- *Jerry*

Shelby: *right now?*

- *hes been crashing in my bed I could smell him on my sheets*

Shelby: *UG wash them*

- *I will believe me*

Shelby: *Rankin has me demo-ing the 10 basic moves. LOL*

- *Can u handle it???*

Shelby: *What because I'm a girl?*

- *No – duh – joking! LOL*

Shelby: *Me too, duh! I wrote THINK WRESTLING on the white board - cool right?*

- *Very*

"You want to know why they don't want 'rastling in the Olympics?" asks Jerry.

I look up from my phone.

"Jerry, change the subject," says my mother. "And by the way, it's pronounced wrestling, not 'rastling."

"Let me tell the kid a few facts," he says. "Facts I read in the paper. I don't write the paper so don't blame me. The reason nobody wants 'rastling in the Olympics is nobody wants to watch grown men roll around in those little bathing suits."

195

"Singlets," corrects my mother. "The uniforms are called singlets. I should know, I bought enough of them."

Jerry comes around to the back of the truck. He rips a wing off the chicken and shoves the piece in his mouth. "That's what I read," he laughs. "It's just too much man-on-man for the American public." He pulls a clean bone from his mouth and flicks it in the grass.

"It's not all guys," I say.

"That's right," chimes my mother. "There's a girl on Mike's team."

Jerry pulls another bone from his mouth. "I guess beating a girl makes Mikey boy feel like a man."

"No, that's how *you* would feel," I say.

Wearing a wide grin, like something is so funny, he steps closer to me. "I wouldn't mind 'rastling with some young lady wearing a singlet."

"Give it a rest," I say.

"Tell you what." Jerry winks at my mother. "I'll box and you wrestle. Let's see who wins."

I keep my eyes on my phone. "Forget it," I say. "I don't need the practice."

"This ain't practice," he says. "This is me and you mixing it up, having some mano a mano."

I ignore him or at least try.

"Annie," says Jerry, "I think you're son is gonna cry." He makes fists and rubs his eyes imitating a baby. Then, he laughs. Not a little laugh, but a gut-busting belly laugh. "Don't worry little Mikey. I wouldn't hurt you."

"Come on guys," says my mother, waving her arm. "That's enough. Let's all eat. Mike, try one of those biscuits."

Jerry reaches into the cooler next to the wheel of the truck and pokes my stomach with his elbow. "Oh, excuse me," he says.

My insides begin to boil. Everything is falling apart because of this asshole and I've had enough of him. I fling my paper plate into the bed of his truck and step in front of him.

He coughs out a dusty sounding laugh. "What's this, the big-shot 'rastler wants to mix it up?"

I raise my fists. "Let's go."

"Jerry, stop it," shouts my mother. "That's enough."

"I win, you stay here and take care of your mother," he says. "You win, you go back to the good witch of the north." He pokes my chest. "Okay, is that a deal?" He pokes me again. "Come on, make a move. You're supposed to be such a tough guy. You got yourself kicked out of school, didn't you?"

"Jerry, he could hurt you," shouts my mother, straining around in her chair. "We're not young anymore."

"Why do you always have to be an asshole," I spit. "Huh, why?"

When he tries to hook his hand over my neck, I set my back foot, turn and hit him with a quick short right-hand. My fist crashes into his jaw. He goes down, rolls, gets up and comes running at me. I duck, sink my shoulder into his stomach and kick out his leg. We crash to the grass. I scramble for control, get on top and position for a cradle. I snag his leg and electric pain shoots down my spine. He has my hair in his fist.

"Now what are you going to do?" he shouts.

My scalp is on fire. I reach, find his balls, grab them and squeeze.

"Say uncle," I spit. "Say it." He pops me in the face with his knee. I squeeze harder.

"Uncle," he screams. "Uncle."

I release him and hop to my feet.

"This is exactly what I didn't want," cries my mother. "And you started it Jerry. You couldn't be nice. I begged you, but you couldn't do it for me."

Holding my bloody nose, my eyes go dead on with my mothers. "I'm outta here," I mouth. "Enjoy your boyfriend."

Jerry, still leaning over holding his nuts, goes to the cooler, fishes around and opens a can of beer. "Annie, you want a beer?" he asks loudly. "One isn't going to hurt the baby."

There is a momentary silence. I look at her. She grimaces then gives me a sheepish smile.

Jerry turns to me. His voice is low and soft, his neck and face splotched pink and red. "Oh, now I did it, didn't I? Mike isn't supposed to know about the baby."

I run two long blocks on Reef Avenue to Central. I sprint through the Wal-Mart's parking lot and into an alley that ends along side the Coral Bridge. I cross a green water canal where alligators wait in the reeds. For a half mile, I parallel Beach Drive. I'm still running hard when a dog charges off a porch. I kick up my heels and leave it in the middle of the road. I follow a path around Fresh Meadows Duck Pond and exit onto a block of neat ranch houses with sprinklers snapping in half circles. Ahead the high school looms at the end of a circular drive.

I slow to a walk and blow blood from my nostrils into the street.

Daylight is fading fast. I jog up a driveway that leads around the school's auditorium. From across the teacher's parking lot, I recognize Mr. Simon, my ninth grade English teacher. I call his name, wave and walk quickly across the striped asphalt squares.

He looks the same, wire-rimmed glasses and too much gel. I was one of the guys in his back row, always cracking jokes, rarely paying any attention.

"It's me," I say. "Mike Brooks."

The teacher doesn't move.

"I had you in ninth grade."

"Didn't you graduate?"

"No, I transferred."

"Yes," he says. "I remember you. The wrestler, second in the States."

Relief comes like cool water on my neck. "Yes, that's me. I was wondering if Coach Juri is still in his office."

"You didn't hear the news?"

I wait.

"He took a position at Southeastern, moved up to college to coach wrestling. It happened fast. When the offer came, he couldn't turn it down."

Stunned, trying to process the information, I remember a

cruel prank; Mr. Simon furious at the blackboard, the back of his pants wet from Coca Cola poured on his chair. I didn't think it was funny.

I ask, "Could I get his phone number?"

The teacher studies me for a moment. "Are you in trouble?"

I follow his eyes to my blood-soaked shirt. "I'm visiting my mother," I say. "I had a fight with her boyfriend."

The teacher wets his lips. "A fight?"

"It's a crazy situation," I say trying to make my voice light. "She broke her ankle and tonight I found out she's having a baby." The words tumble from my lips. "You see, she told me that I needed to come back here to help out. I thought she ended it with her boyfriend. If I could talk to Coach Juri it would...." I trail off. It would what?

The teacher unclips his phone from his belt. "I'll call the police for you."

"No, don't do that," I say. "It's over. I'm fine now."

He removes his car keys from his suit pants pocket. "Well, I have to be someplace and I'm already late. Come back tomorrow after school. You can meet the new coach. He'll be here." The teacher snaps the locks open on a small silver compact. "Good to see you again and good luck with your mother and the new sibling."

Chapter 23

AFTER ABOUT TWENTY TEXTS with Tara and twenty minutes later, I arrive at the Atlantic View Hotel. Tara has rented a room and thrown Tie-Dye Luke an afternoon birthday party. I go around back to the patio that meets the hard Daytona sand. A warm wind brings the sound of breaking waves. For a few minutes, I watch Tara streaking back and forth in the hotel's pool. Each time her long tan body reaches the side, she does a quick half somersault and kicks off.

I squat at the side of the pool. She swims over and hooks her elbows on the wet cement edge. Her slicked-back hair shines under the patio spotlights that dance on the blue water. "You made it," she says.

"Yeah, I walked from the high school."

"Why didn't you Uber?" She springs from the pool; tall, slim, bikini dripping, skin goose pimply from the breeze. She places her fingertips on the sides of my swollen nose and examines it like a doctor. "What happened to you? Not another fight?"

"I didn't start it."

"You never do."

"Lay off. I'm not in the mood."

"You ruined your shirt."

"It was old anyway."

"I can't believe you're back." She slips her wet arms around me and kisses my lips. Her body is cool and firm. I remember nights on the beach. Nights when I couldn't stop kissing and wanting her.

"You stopped returning my texts," she says. "I thought I was supposed to visit you?"

I swallow. "I didn't know moving would be so hard."

"I didn't know if I'd hear from you again."

What do I say except I'm sorry, but saying that would be a lie.

"You missed the party," she says. "We cut school and started early. Tie-Dye is still in the room." She wraps herself in a white hotel towel with a blue stripe down the middle.

"Could I crash there tonight?" I ask.

"I doubt you'd want to."

"Don't tell me you and Tie-Dye?" My heart waits in mid-beat.

"No, I'm not into him like that." She shoves her finger down her throat and fake gags. "Kyle Scruggs is up there."

My spine stiffens. Did she really say, Kyle Scruggs? I haven't seen him since the day of our fight.

"Don't worry," she says. "He's mellowed out." She picks up a pair of shorts from a lounge. "So what's going on? Why didn't you tell me you were coming back to Daytona?"

What's going on? My mother is pregnant. I'm going to have a brother or sister. I like a girl named Shelby Hoffman. I say,

"My mother broke her ankle. I'm supposed to be here to help her out."

"Oh, crap, that stinks." Under the towel, Tara tugs her wet bikini bottoms off her thighs, past her knees. She steps out of them and drops the tiny roll of material on a glass-topped table.

I watch her pull on her shorts and slip a Hooters t-shirt over her head. She works under it with her hands and somehow removes the wet bathing suit top. Finally, she pushes her feet into leather sandals and takes a fresh towel from a lounge and twirls it on her head like a genie. "Come on," she says taking my hand. "Show's over. I'll take you up to the room."

On the second floor, she leads me down a carpeted hallway and takes out her door key card.

"I'll warn you before we go in," she says. "Tie-Dye drank way too much and got completely wasted. He's sleeping it off."

Tara pushes in and hits the lights. On one bed, Kyle Scruggs leans back on pillows stacked against the headboard. Above his surfer shorts, his chest is tan and wide. In his hand, he's balancing a bottle of Jagermeister. Tie-Dye Luke lies across the foot of the other bed. A blue wetsuit is turned down to his waist. Empty rubberized arms dangle off his sides.

Kyle Scruggs caps the bottle of Jager, puts on a pair of black-rimmed glasses and says, "Who invited him?"

"Me," says Tara. "So chill out."

Right off, I notice there's something funny about his eyes. His pupils don't line up.

He catches me staring. "I'm lucky I can still see out of my

left eye," he says. "The doctor had to take bone from my hip and fuse it to my face. Now my eyes don't move together and I'm stuck wearing these." He takes his glasses off and drops them on the bed.

I stand there, sort of transfixed, looking at the damage I've done. I'm not exactly sure what I'm feeling, but it crashes over me like a wave. "Man, I'm sorry 'bout that."

"You're sorry," he says, sarcastically. "Real sorry, I bet."

"Aw, you can hardly notice it," says Tara.

I lean back on the ledge above the air conditioner knowing I should leave. In a strange way, I'm hoping Kyle punches me in the face. I feel like I deserve it. Tara pokes Tye Dye like he's something dead she found on the beach. He opens one eye and shuts it.

"Kyle doesn't go to our school anymore," she says, squeezing in next to me.

"My parents were waiting for an excuse to get me out of that school," he says. "They stuck me in Tallahassee Military."

"He's learning how to walk in a straight line," says Tara.

"I heard you're wrestling in New Jersey," says Kyle.

"Yeah, still at it," I say. "You still taking Taekwondo?"

"Nah, I had to quit. My doctor said I couldn't take another hit in the face."

I think about Kyle walking around with one eye out of line for the rest of his life. Every photo taken of him will be a reminder of the day Mike Brooks clobbered him with a roundhouse right. I don't want this on me.

Tara unwinds the towel from her head and shakes out her

hair. "It was so hot today," she says. "Like a hundred and ten degrees in that kitchen."

I ask, "What kitchen?"

"Okay, get ready." She smiles and points to her shirt. "I got a job. I'm a waitress at Hooters."

"The place with the little orange shorts," I say.

"Hey," she fake pouts at me. "I had to go through an interview and everything. You just don't walk into Hooters, put on a uniform and start working."

"My mother worked there when it first opened," I say. "She didn't like it."

"Why, because she had to shake her booty sometimes?" asks Tara.

"Something like that," I say and remember my mother coming home in tears. Some college a-hole dumped a drink down her chest and yelled, *Wet t-shirt party.* The manager gave her a new shirt and refused to kick the guy out.

"If the money stays good," says Tara. "I'll take a gap year before starting college."

Kyle holds out the Jager to me.

"Unlike you and me," says Tara, "Mike doesn't drink." She grabs the bottle and shouts, "This is supposed to be a party." She lets out a loud "whoop" that falls flat in the quiet room.

Tye Dye Luke murmurs something and rolls onto his side.

"Birthday boy is still polluted," says Kyle.

Tara takes a swig of Jager and hands the bottle back to Kyle. He takes a big swallow and caps it.

"Last Saturday night I made a hundred in tips," says Tara.

"I spent it on this stupid party." She secures a red Solo cup between her thighs and finds a bottle of wine on the floor. She pours some into the cup. "Luckily, I got this room half price. You know that weird guy with the long hair who wears Pearl Jam shirts to school?" She pushes my shoulder and laughs. "He works the desk here and has had a crush on me since the sixth grade."

"The guitar guy who tries to sing like Eddie Vetter?" asks Kyle.

Tara snorts out a laugh. "Exactly, exactly." She gulps the wine like she's thirsty.

Kyle snaps open a knapsack at the side of the bed and pulls out a fat zip-lock baggie of weed.

I've never seen so much pot. All my mother ever had was a few bony joints in her cigarette pack.

I want to ask Tara how things could change so quickly for her. Tie-Dye Luke and Kyle Scruggs? Hooters? All Tie-Dye ever did was lurk around the corners of the school in a cloud of smoke. And, Kyle is one of the top two reasons I left Florida.

"Should I tell Mike who has the best pot in Volusia County?" asks Tara.

Kyle starts rolling a joint. "Don't go blowing the dude up," he says.

"He should know," she says. "The guy is dating his mother."

"Jerry?" I ask

Kyle finds his phone on the nightstand and holds it out to me. "That's where you used to live, right?" he asks.

I read my address on Google Maps.

"Dude, your neighborhood is completely sketchy," he says.

"You bought weed from Jerry at my house?" I ask.

He laughs, "I thought you moved."

"It's still his house," says Tara.

I picture Jerry opening the front door, CAT diesel cap pulled low, tooth pick in his lips, wife beater showing off his muscled arms, his wallet fat with bills. My head seems to expand and snap back into place.

Kyle watches me with his screwed up eyes. "Don't get bent about it," he says. "The guy has good shit and good prices."

I get this trapped feeling. My hands go clammy. It's like I'm covered with ants, like the room is a nest. I get up. Tara snags my arm. I shake her off and head to the door.

"Mike, come on, hang out," she calls.

In the hall, I bolt past the elevator and charge down the stairs. The hotel's lobby is empty. I close my eyes and take deep breaths. I want to, need to be back in Molly Pitcher.

I call my aunt and listen to her phone ring until her message clicks on. Then, I'm getting a call.

"Honey, where are you?" asks my mother.

"Is Jerry selling marijuana from our house?" My voice is trembling.

"Who told you that?"

"Is he?"

"Mike, it's a little pot for some extra money."

"He's sold to my friends. You could go to jail."

"You're being dramatic," she says.

"Ma, are you crazy. You're pregnant, right?" I stare at dead electrical beer signs on a pine-paneled wall.

"I'm sorry you found out like that."

"You need to get away from him. We both know he's going to be a terrible father."

I hear her breathing, composing. "Mike, honey, listen," she says. "I've been waiting for the right moment to bring this up. What I am about to say is good news. It's something I want. Something Jerry and I want. We have a trip planned to Vegas."

"So what. Cancel it."

"We booked one of those Elvis Presley chapel weddings, pink Cadillac convertible and everything."

I tip my head up to the water-stained ceiling tiles and gulp air. "No, please don't marry him."

She goes on explaining that Jerry's divorce is final and if she gets married she'd be on his medical coverage. "Do you know how much it costs to have a baby?" she asks.

"He's dealing weed from our house," I growl.

"For the time being only," she says. "And isn't it legal or something?"

I want to throw my phone. "Not in Florida."

"Well, I can't worry about that right now because what am I supposed to do? He's keeping me afloat. I'm in no position to complain. You and I both know my sister doesn't need a baby and me." She forces a laugh. "Try to imagine that."

"Jerry is never going to change." I pace the lobby, one hand squeezing my temples, the other holding the phone. "He'll hate the baby and he'll hate you for having it."

"No, it will be his own blood."

"Oh and I'm not so he picks a fight with me and rips a clump of hair out of my head?"

"I didn't like what happened today," she says. "I'm very upset with the way he treated you. I spoke to him and he wants to talk to you. He's taking responsibility."

"Mom, wake up. Jerry's not five years old."

"And I'm not twenty-five anymore," she says. "Having a baby at my age is a big deal. I'm not doing it alone."

"You wouldn't be alone."

"Mike, I have a chance to keep this house."

"Do you want the baby?" I ask.

Silence.

"Do you?"

"I think I do."

"You don't. You couldn't want anything of his."

"Mike, honey-."

"Stop calling me that," I seethe. "If you cared about me, you wouldn't have gone back with him. You wouldn't have lied to get me down here."

Tara, hair still wet and long on her shoulders, comes up the hall holding the wine bottle by the neck. She changed her shirt to a tie-dye with a big peace sign on the chest.

"Mom, I have to go," I say.

"Are you coming home?"

Jerry is in the background, then he's on the phone. "Mike, you're making your mother very upset. Stop playing games and get your ass home."

I end the call.

Hands tight on the steering wheel of Tara's Nissan, my foot slamming the gas, I speed past hulking hotels, chain restaurants and blazing billboards. Tara is playing with the radio, changing stations. My phone is blowing up with calls and texts from my mother.

"That's where I work!" Tara points at a Hooters sign with the owl logo. "Do you want to get some hot wings? I get an employee discount."

I'm hungry, but there's no way I could sit in a restaurant and eat. Get my backpack and leave Florida, that's all I'm thinking. At the airport, I'll call my aunt and have her buy my plane ticket. I don't care if I have to sleep on the floor of the terminal. As a matter of fact, I'm looking forward to it. I exit the bright boulevard and merge onto a four-lane highway. "Watch for cops," I say. "I don't have a driver's license."

"You don't?"

"No."

"Then pull over. I'll drive."

"You were drinking."

"This is my car," she huffs. "And besides, what are you going to do if we see a cop car?"

I have no idea. I goose the accelerator, throwing her back in the seat.

Jerry's truck is angle parked across the front yard. Lights are on in the house. I pull past the truck and kill the engine.

Tara takes a swig of wine. "Just hurry up," she says. "You're like murdering my buzz."

Outside, the air purrs with frog bellows and thrumming crickets. Across the street, through gauzy curtains, a TV flashes Monday Night Football. I follow a moonlit path into my backyard. Through the open window, I hear Jerry say, "Like I'm supposed to know they were Mike's friends?"

"They were kids," says my mother. "Anyone could see that. So stop selling to kids."

"I do know one thing," he shouts. "I'm the one sticking my neck out. I don't see you taking chances."

"Mike?"

Heart stuffed in my throat, I spin around.

"There were mosquitoes in the car. One bit my ankle," says Tara.

"Be quiet," I say, shushing her.

She scratches her leg. "So you're going to stand out here all night at the window?"

"I don't know. Maybe until Jerry leaves."

Tara steps away and pukes on the ground. She goes into a dry heave then straightens up. "Too many Doritos," she says, wiping her mouth on her arm.

I wonder how to play this. Maybe I should just leave my backpack and clothes behind and drive to the airport. I could call my aunt on the ride there. But, what do I do with Tara? I can't let her drive. She's absolutely too drunk.

"Where did that come from?" She eyes Jerry's new

building. Light seeps from under the garage door and around the front window. She crosses a thicket of overgrown weeds and tries to look in the window. "Mike, come over here," she calls. "It smells funny, like something is burning."

I jam my index finger to my lips and widen my eyes at her.

"Come over here," she hisses.

I smell it. Something is burning.

We walk the perimeter of the steel building, turn at the far end and stop at an air conditioner jutting from a window. Around it, smoke curls into the dead night air.

"Be careful," says Tara.

I hold the sides of the unit, hoist myself up and look into the smoky window. Lights blaze above rows of two-foot plants in plastic buckets. In the far corner, sparks shoot from a wall outlet and something is on fire.

"What the hell is this?" I say, half to myself.

When I lean in closer to get a better look, the air conditioner wobbles, tips from the window and crashes to the ground.

"Are you alright?" asks Tara.

I hop to my feet and feel my heart pounding. "We have to get out of here."

"Why, what's in there?"

"He's growing grass."

"Grass?"

"Marijuana."

A thunderous boom hits me hard as a speeding car. The next thing I know, I'm rolling into the soft marsh grass at the edge of the yard. I lie there for about a minute with my ears ringing, then get to my feet and stagger across the grass looking for Tara. Pieces of the building crash down around me. Flames leap and roar into the night sky.

Chapter 24

TWO DAYS LATER, it's a miracle. I'm in Jersey standing on the arrival's deck at Newark Airport searching for a bus to carry me south on the Turnpike, south on the Garden State, then even further south to Molly Pitcher. Hand in my pocket on my last twenty-dollar bill, I'm flooded with relief and so looking forward to seeing Shelby and getting back on the wrestling mat.

I snap a selfie in front of the United Airlines sign and text it to her.

A moment later: ☺ *can't wait!!!*

I call my aunt to let her know I've landed safely. She's about to lead a marathon aerobics class and couldn't get away from the gym to pick me up.

"I made it," I say.

"How was your flight?"

"They served peanuts and a free drink. I was happy."

"I was so worried," she says with relief in her voice. "You're sure you're okay with taking the bus? I could ask Tony to drive out there."

"I'll figure it out."

"Then I'll see you tonight at the house. The key is in the mailbox where it always is. I'm cooking a nice dinner for us. How does that sound?"

I tell her it sounds great.

It takes me twenty minutes to find the bus that stops in Molly Pitcher. I pay the driver and slide into the last row next to the window. Tired to my bones, I shut my eyes and rest my head back as the bus accelerates and rumbles from the airport. My ears ring a bit, and my eyes begin to close, as I give in to exhaustion.

It's a restless sleep. The explosion flashes in my mind, flames roar and fire curls into the sky. It dances up the walls of my house and leaps into the windows. Furniture catches and bursts into flames. Curtains drip like they were made of wax. The fire department with their trucks, hoses and grim faces watch the fire shoot twenty feet into the black sky.

I wake with a jolt. The bus zooms past the green sign for Exit 13A.

None of what happened feels real anymore. Tara, my mother and I were taken to the hospital by ambulance. My mother had her ankle looked at and re-casted. Tara broke her pinky finger. I got away with a massive headache and ringing in my ears. The doctor said we were all very lucky. Of course, Jerry didn't get a scratch. Two policemen questioned me at the hospital. They were pretty chill about the whole thing. They said there was evidence that Jerry was starting a large-scale marijuana-grow house. Chemical containers, fertilizer bags, charred pots and blackened grow lights were recovered from the fire. "You did us a favor," one joked. "You put him out of business."

The night of the fire, Tara's parents let me crash on their couch. With the family's basset hound wheezing and sneezing in his bed, I laid awake missing Shelby, my aunt and my new life in Jersey. I wanted it back.

The bus stops in a parking lot across from a familiar looking church. People jostle their bags from the overhead. I make my way down the main aisle.

"Is this Molly Pitcher?" I ask.

"It was yesterday," says the driver.

With nothing except the clothes on my back and my phone in my pocket, I step off the bus and run into the wind. My chest expands with each breath of cold air. Slowly, my body warms. I cross a bridge over a highway and follow a curving road past withered cornfields that stretch to an unpainted barn. I maintain a steady pace until I reach the center of town.

I arrive at the high school with ten minutes left in the day's last class. Still huffing, I try the gym doors, the custodian's door and then the band doors. All locked. Two women in white aprons talk on a cement sally port outside the cafeteria. Behind them, a delivery entrance leads into the school's kitchen.

"You can't go in there," shouts one of the women.

I dash past them, wind my way around the ovens and stainless steel tables and enter the empty cafeteria. After the final bell, Shelby's sure to go to the gym to get ready for practice. I want to be there waiting for her. I walk quickly up the science hall and jog through the lobby. The gym doors are chocked open. I enter and inhale the soft smell of wax on the polished floor. I made it. I'm back.

Light shines from under Coach Rankin's door. I knock gently, ease the door open a few inches and stick my head in. "It's me," I say. "I'm back."

The coach shuts a newspaper and lifts his glasses on top of his freckled scalp. "So you did return," he says surprised. "How's your mother? How's her ankle?"

"She's getting around on crutches." I think about the other news, the bigger news, I'm going to have a brother or sister.

"And how are you?" asks Rankin.

I can't help smiling. "Glad to be here."

"We need to talk." The coach wags a finger at a chair. "Because here's the thing, I didn't expect you so soon. To tell the truth, I didn't know if you were ever returning. Adjustments were made. So, you'll need to be patient."

I keep my eyes on the old coach. "Adjustments?"

He gives me a cheerless look. "I'm not saying this is your fault. No one is saying that, but you leaving put a hole in the roster and left the team without a starter."

"But I'm back in time for the match," I say. "I told you I would be."

"I wish it were that simple. It's been decided that Zach Goochinov will start at 138, at least for this weekend's matches."

I can't believe what I'm hearing. "I only missed three days."

The coach's patient face doesn't move.

"You saw the way Gooch acted when he lost to Shelby. Doesn't that matter?"

Still the coach says nothing.

"Isn't this week the Trojans?" I ask. "The great and all powerful Andrew Fox. Last year's state champ."

"Look Mike, there's some politics going on," replies Rankin. "I'm not going to deny it."

"What does that mean?"

"It means, Gooch wrestles this weekend and-."

I cut in, "Do you think that's fair?"

"Fair?" He waggles his head. "No, it's not fair and I probably shouldn't be having this conversation with you. I'm supposed to tell you that Gooch worked hard this week and earned the spot back. That's what I'm supposed to tell you."

"It's a quad, right?" I say, not giving up. "That's three matches. Let me wrestle Fox? Gooch can take the other two matches."

"Mike, I can't."

"Can't?"

"No. There were some," he purses his lips, "some allowances made. It's been decided that Gooch will earn his matches for his varsity standing."

"So he'll qualify for a letter?"

The coach nods. "Yes."

"So Gooch's father talked to Principal Hoffman and-."

The coach raises his hand. "Don't go there. What's done is done and you will live to wrestle another day."

I push back in the chair. "What if Gooch wins and doesn't want to give up the weight class. Do I get to wrestle him off?"

Rankin crosses his arms. "Mike, it's complicated. There's history and undercurrents at work. Gooch's father has supported our program for four years and wants his son to earn his letter. It means a great deal to him."

"And wrestling means a lot to me," I say.

"I know that and you'll get your matches." His face has a pitying look and I hate it.

"Aren't you in charge of the team?" I ask.

"Technically, yes, I am. But, someday you'll realize, no one is ever fully in charge. We all have a boss."

I stand and shove the chair into the wall.

"Let's get through this weekend," he says. "And see what happens."

"That's it, that's your plan?" I say. "See what happens?"

"For now," he says. "And one more thing, you were officially absent from school today, so you can't practice."

"Aw, come on," I whine.

"If it was up to me, I'd let you join in."

"But nothing's up to you, is it?" I punch his white board. It crashes to the floor. A second later I'm out his door. Three days away and I've been replaced. My gut is a knot of frustrated anger. I cross the gym and bang open an exit door.

"Mike!"

I look back.

219

Shelby drops her gym bag and runs toward me, almost sprints the space between us. "What's wrong?" she asks. "Is it your mother?"

"No, it's not my mother."

"Is she okay?"

"She was planning to get married in Vegas by Elvis," I spit.

"Wow, to Jerry?"

"Yeah, but like I told you our house burnt down." I hear my own words. Saying them makes it too real.

Outside, in the waning afternoon, we find a corner of the school where the bricks have absorbed the sun's heat. Backs on the wall, knees bent, the soles of our Nikes on the rough asphalt, we sit shoulder to shoulder. Shelby says she wants to hear everything from the beginning.

"Won't you be late for practice?" I ask.

"We have ten minutes," she says.

Where do I start? How? She knows most of it through texts and rushed conversations. I haven't told her my mother is pregnant. Just thinking about Jerry being a father twists me with rage. I begin with Tara smelling smoke in my yard. Shelby listens wide-eyed and it feels so good to be next to her. Good to get the story out of me. I describe the explosion and how the building lifted and broke apart. I tell her the fire leapt to my house like it was alive. "Flames were going up the drapes and across the walls. And get this," I say. "As I'm carrying my mother out of the house, Jerry runs past, jumps into his truck and drives it up the block."

"So you saved your mother?" she asks.

I don't mind being a hero in her eyes. "Yeah, and Jerry saved his truck."

"Did he come back to the house?"

"He tried to put the fire out with the garden hose. It was too hot. The metal building in the yard actually melted."

"Wait," says Shelby. "Back up. Did you say Tara, your old girlfriend, was there?"

I sigh. "I needed a ride to my house. I didn't have a car."

"Very convenient," says Shelby. "Is Tara visiting you for Christmas?"

"I know what you're getting at, but nothing happened."

"It's fine if it did," she says. "She was your girlfriend or still could be."

"Shelby, come on."

"I saw what she looks like."

"You're worried because she's skinny?" I ask.

"Not just skinny, try tall, skinny and pretty."

"Shelby, you've got everything going on."

"You don't think I'm too muscular?"

"No, not at all." I take her hand. We intertwine fingers.

"I'm terrible," she says. "I mean, you just had your house burn down."

I think about having no house to return to, nothing to show for my seventeen years on this earth. Where I grew up, slept, ate my meals and looked out my window, there are only black charred walls. My dad's photo albums and the flag from his military burial are ashes. What do I have that proves he ever existed? And then there is the unborn baby my mother is carrying inside her. Tears start in my eyes. How will that baby have a chance without me?

"Hey," says Shelby. "Are you okay?"

I inhale and shut my eyes.

"If you need anything," she says. "I have some money saved."

"It's not about money." I let out a measured breath. I have to tell her and wonder why I feel ashamed. What am I ashamed of? I shudder deep in my chest. "My mother is pregnant and she's not taking care of herself."

"Pregnant?"

"Jerry is the father." I am so full of shame and embarrassment, I begin to tremble.

She squeezes my hand in both of hers. "Does your aunt know?"

"Yeah."

Shelby doesn't have to say anything because I know what she's thinking. Having a baby should be a totally good thing, but this time it's not.

Chapter 25

THE QUAD is going to be a full house. People are filling the bleachers, sitting shoulder to shoulder. Everyone is excited, pointing iPhones, snapping photos of the wrestlers. Cheerleaders in bright uniforms wave pom-poms and shout, "Be Aggressive! B-E Aggressive!"

I slump at the top of the bleachers looking over the standing-room-only crowd. I'm not dressed for the quad, because I'm not wrestling. Coach Rankin said I could dress and sit on the team bench. "For what?" I'd snapped. "So I can watch Gooch?"

I feel like a ghost, like my presence in the gym is totally random. If I disappeared right now, who would care or notice?

One of our guys is on the mat getting a wrestling lesson from the 126-pound Trojan wrestler. Each time he faces his Trojan opponent, he's taken down for two points, then let up again. He does earn one point for the escape, but the math isn't in his favor. It's obvious the Trojan is trying for a Technical Fall, which ends the match when he's fifteen points ahead. Shelby has the next match at 132-pounds. Just thinking about it raises the sweat in my armpits, that's how bad I want her to win.

My phone buzzes:

Shelby: *where r u - gooch is missing - rankin is going nuts*

I shoot to my feet and scan the throngs of spectators and wrestlers. My eyes find Shelby near the girl's locker room. She's in full uniform: skullcap, headgear and singlet. Beside her, Principal Hoffman shakes someone's hand.

I stomp down the bleachers and work my way to her.

"Did you call Gooch?" I ask.

She sort of smirks. "He was flipping out last night. And you know why?" She nods toward the corner of the gym.

I follow her eyes to Andrew Fox, pacing the sidelines. He's muscled as a pit bull, thick from his ankles to his non-existent neck.

Coach Rankin clamps a hand on my shoulder. "I'm looking for Gooch," he says. "He was here this morning for weigh-ins and I haven't seen him since."

Shelby and I shake our heads.

"Mike, do me a favor. Scout around the area. If you see him, tell me. I'll handle it from there. Can you do that for me?"

I shrug an okay.

Gooch isn't in the locker room. I check under the stall doors in the lavatory. Some kid is stinking the place up, but it isn't Gooch. I circle the gym and walk the hallway, past the admission's table to the exit doors. Gooch's Mustang is in the parking lot against the fence. No one is in the car.

In the JV gym, where the Booster Club sells nachos, hotdogs, pretzels, meatball heroes and drinks, I find him on a bench with a white towel draped over his lowered head.

I push his shoulder. "The coach is looking for you."

From under the towel, he mutters, "Got drunk last night." He gives a small laugh. "Made grilled cheese sandwiches with pickles at like one in the morning."

"And you're admitting this to me?" I say.

He tries to laugh. "Why not? It's the truth."

I look around and think about walking away, but say, "Go tell the coach you quit on the team, because you sure don't want to wrestle."

"Maybe I will." He removes the towel from his head and rubs it on his face. "You checked him out?"

"Who?"

"Andrew Fox."

"Yeah, he's warming up."

"A horror movie, right?"

Cheers and applause from the main gym drift in. Shelby's match is being announced.

"You want to know what I don't understand?" asks Gooch. "Why didn't Rankin put her at 138? The whole team knows I'm solid at 132. At least I'd guarantee one win."

"You'd rather have Shelby wrestle Fox?" I ask.

"Why not? No one expects a girl to win. When she blows the match, it's the ultimate excuse."

I glare at Gooch. "Man, grow a set of balls."

His black eyebrows rise on his pale forehead. "You're saying that to me? You show up and expect to be taken in, put on varsity, put on a pedestal like you're some kind of wrestling superhero. You haven't earned anything here. And now you're

225

probably looking forward to me getting destroyed by Fox."

"Better you than Shelby," I spit.

"I saw you with her."

"So what. We're friends."

"Why lie about it? It's so obvious. The entire school knows you've been trying to hook up with her from day one. You could have had Janice, but she wasn't good enough. Even when I told you Shelby was mine, you didn't stop."

I force a laugh. "Shelby makes her own decisions."

"So now you're going to tell me about Shelby," he blurts, rolling his eyes. "Because I know everything about her."

Again, the crowd roars.

"So then you know she's like me," I say. "She doesn't like to lose."

He laughs. "You know what, you can have her. I've been there and done that."

I'd like to slap the conceited grin off his face. I hold steady. He isn't worth it. Let him get obliterated by Fox. Let him get pinned in fifteen seconds in front of the whole town. "Don't bother warming up," I say. "Because Fox is going to rip you a new one no matter what you do."

"Tell Rankin to find another human sacrifice. I'm done for today."

"Tell him yourself," I say.

In the gym, I'm assaulted by fans pounding their feet on the bleachers and chanting, "Shell-bee, Shell-bee."

I cut through the crowd to the edge of the mat and there she is - flat out, chest on chest, over the 132-pound Trojan wrestler, her calf muscles knotted, her thighs trembling, her face vibrating from strain. The Trojan wrestler bucks side to side, but can't break Shelby's arm bar.

I check the clock. Fifteen seconds left in the first period.

Tendons rise in her neck. A single vein pumps over her balled bicep. She is magnificent. One-hundred and thirty-two pounds of hard, trembling muscle.

I cup my mouth and shout, "Squeeze it and lift his head." I don't know if she can hear me, but I have to yell it. "Shelby, lift his head, lift it!"

She secures her grip and pulls the Trojan's head off the mat forcing his shoulders down.

The ref's hand slaps flat. His whistle sounds. It's over.

She has pinned! Pinned at her weight class!

She leaps to her feet, tears off her headgear and stands center of the mat, smiling, soaking in the applause. I rush the mat with the rest of the team. Everyone on the Molly Pitcher side of the gym is standing and applauding.

"You did it," I shout.

I'm about to hug her when Coach Rankin takes my elbow. "Celebrate later," he says in my ear. "Right now, you have to come with me."

"Where?"

"Come on, we don't have a lot of time."

The coach of the Trojans, a pretty woman with a man's haircut and dangly gold earrings, and a referee in his black and white uniform are waiting at the scale in the boy's locker room.

"What's going on?" I say.

"I cut a deal," says Rankin. "Turns out, Andrew Fox's parents don't want their son's one hundredth win recorded as a forfeit." He smiles. "You have to make weight."

I try to think things out, but my mind has gone numb. "I should take a leak first," I say.

Rankin laughs, "It's one or the other with you."

I enter a stall and lift the seat. I shudder at the last trickle and stare vacantly at the wall. I barely practiced this week. Haven't stretched, didn't sleep well. "Is this really happening?" I whisper.

Back at the scale, I kick off my sneakers. The numbers flash to 140.

"He's two over," says the ref.

I pull off my t-shirt, unsnap my jeans and drop them. I'm wearing an old pair of boxer briefs that I'd never wear if I knew I was weighing in. The elastic is wavy as cooked bacon. In socks and underwear, I step back on the scale. The digits settle at 138.

"Perfect," says the Trojans' coach. "We have ourselves a match."

I gather my clothes and hold them in my arms.

Coach Rankin hangs back. "Mike, you want this, don't you?"

I swallow an uneasy feeling and say, "I wouldn't want Andrew Fox reaching one hundred wins on a forfeit."

The coach places one foot on a bench and leans in close. "I've been watching you and there's something I noticed. You actually love it, don't you?"

"You mean wrestling?" I ask.

"What else," he says. "So here's some advice, go out there and do what you love. Do what you've worked for. Wrestle and know this day, this time, this single match will never come again. Shaved head or no shaved head, Andrew Fox is no different than all the rest."

"Maybe different because he's never lost," I say.

"Which makes him cocky," says Rankin. "He's wearing his perfect record around his neck like a two-hundred pound anchor. That record is the chink in his armor. He's thinking you're more meat to chew and spit out. Surprise him. You're the unknown, the stranger riding into town on a dark horse." The coach's eyes are hungry and bright. "He'll be impatient. Use that. Work with that. Frustrate him. Make him wrestle your match."

I jam my clothes in my locker. "I need to forget he's never lost," I say.

"Get this in your head," says Rankin. "Today is Andrew Fox's first loss. Now go out and make it a reality. Show every one in this town what you love to do."

Rankin holds out his hand.

I take it.

"Show them," he says. "Do it for yourself and do it for me, your coach."

Alone in the locker room, I slip my feet into my singlet and pull the straps over my shoulders. I straighten my underwear and adjust my junk, so it's not all bunched up. I wonder if I should say a prayer. Some of the guys in Daytona prayed before matches. I don't know any actual prayers. I've never been in a church. I lower my head. "Maybe today, just this once, you could watch over me." I'm about to tie my shoelaces when I remember my mother and the baby. "Skip that," I whisper. "Keep your eyes on my mother and my new brother or sister."

Chapter 26

WHEN I STEP ONTO THE MAT, a hush falls over the rowdy fans. Andrew Fox levels his eyes at me. His face holds nothing resembling an emotion. His cauliflowered ears stick out from his shaved head like fungi. His hollow cheeks, bare head and white skin are so alien, a wave of nausea rises into my throat. He straps on his headgear and swings his muscled arms like fisted clubs.

I feel cold and unprepared. I touch my toes and shut my eyes. "No fear," I whisper. "No doubts. Be quick. Be strong. Be focused."

Someone in the away-side bleacher shouts, "Go back to Florida."

People clap, cheer and boo.

I step to the center circle. The ref mumbles something about keeping it clean. "Got that?" he asks.

Fox eyes me up and down.

I look for Shelby and find her at the edge of the mat. She mouths something, maybe, "You can do it."

I shake hands with Fox, toe the line and take my stance. My mind races over a game plan - play off him, let him shoot, let him make mistakes.

The whistle sounds.

Fox launches like a leopard, clamps my ankle and springs to his feet. Three seconds in and I'm hopping on one foot, trying to keep my balance. Not a good start. The roar from the stands comes in a tidal wave of sound.

Coach Rankin yells, "Whizzer! Whizzer!"

But, it's too late. My support leg is kicked out. I tumble face first to the mat with Fox on my back. He's earned a two-point takedown.

The pace is too quick. I must slow it down. He's an octopus on steroids, locking in my legs and pulling at my arms.

Think.

Inhale.

Exhale.

Breathe.

I stay flat on my stomach, every muscle flexed.

"Get to your feet," shouts Rankin. "And wake up!"

Fox works the "boots" in, locking his legs around mine. At the same time, he yanks my left arm behind my back. I rise on one hand and one knee. I kick my left leg free and, with a twisting turn, drop my weight. We roll across the mat.

Fox releases me. I'm free.

The ref raises one finger for my escape. Fox leads two to one.

We square off and lock up. I work my hands for an inside position. Fox's arms are steel cables, inflexible. His body, already slippery with sweat, jerks right, then left. I hold on.

The ref breaks us apart. We take our stances in the center circle.

At the whistle, we lock up again. Fox's strength won't allow a move. I can't make him yield. His shot comes out of nowhere. A single outside leg. I push into him, instead of away, and wrap my arm around his smooth head. I get a solid hold and tighten a horse collar. We are straining and breathing hard. I can't move him. Seconds pass.

The whistle.

Stalemate.

I have to think, get a move in my head. Didn't I tell Shelby it's called, Think Wrestling? But nothing comes, no strategy except react and survive.

Center mat, the whistle sounds. We tie up. Fox snakes one arm behind my neck. His other arm is locked on my wrist. He shoots.

I sprawl and land hard on his neck and shoulders.

The buzzer sounds. Period one is over. Fox leads, 2 to 1.

Rankin cups his hands to his mouth and shouts, "Down position."

Center of the circle, I kneel and place my palms on the mat. Rankin wants me to earn another point for an escape, which would tie the score. Fox leans over me.

I remember what I told Shelby. Two sticks of dynamite. Explode up. Explode.

The whistle. I burst up and drag Fox along. Twisting and working his fingers apart, I trot in a circle, careful not to step out of bounds. On the second turn around the mat, I kick forward. Fox loses his grip. The ref awards me one point for my escape.

The crowd noise swells. The chant, "Fox, Fox, Fox!" echoes throughout the gym.

We face off.

Fox shoots and wraps his arms around my knee.

Then, what I have been waiting for, unknowingly looking for, is in front of me. The match seems to slow. The move hangs there, waiting for me to act.

Spladle.

Yes, Fox is open for the dreaded spladle. No one spladles a state champ. Should I even try? He won't expect it. Never see it coming. It's a ballsy move, so ballsy. I bend over his back, grab his knee and thread my right leg behind his left ankle.

He must sense the move coming. He bucks trying to escape. I roll, bringing him with me, burying the back of his pink-shaved head in my gut and force his legs into the air.

I have hooked and spread Fox's legs apart into a banana split. I'm thinking how the hell did a state champion let me put him in a garbage move like a spladle? Is he going to pull some nasty move and escape? On his back, he struggles and bucks. I hold tight and spladle him like a gymnast doing an inverted split. My old coach's words run through my head, *Position him so that you can plant a tulip in his butt hole.*

The guys had roared with laughter.

I reach and grab Fox's ankle. I adjust my body so I'm on my right side, shoulders raised.

Fox fights, twists, kicks, making it tough for me to finish the move. I place my free leg over his leg and shove my stomach into the back of his head. At the same time, I pull his legs over my body until he looks like he's trying to sniff his own butt.

The ref is flat out, watching for the pin. Fox is practically bent in half, feet dancing in the air like sock puppets. He rocks one side to the other. My muscles turn to stone. For Fox there is nothing left to do except struggle and hope to be saved by the clock. I tilt to my left and ratchet the move a few notches.

Fox lets out a surrendering grunt.

The ref slaps the mat.

It's over.

A wall of cheering, boos and applause floods the gym.

Fox gets to his feet and flings his head gear. His head is a tomato. I wait at the line. Finally, he comes over and gives my hand a quick shake.

The crowd hoots and cheers.

He jogs across the mat and shakes Coach Rankin's hand, then crosses back and kicks a chair, sending it airborne.

The Minutemen swamp me and pound my back. Shelby bear hugs me. She's laughing in my ear, "You did it. You spladled the great Andrew Fox."

Chapter 27

I BANG OUT the school doors in a daze of euphoria. I completed the quad, winning all three matches. The locker room was a crazy scene of yelling and music. Shelby and Janice stormed in for the celebration. Shelby won two of her three matches. Everyone was congratulating her. Coach Rankin told the team to cool it and ordered the girls out, but no one took him seriously. He finally gave up and danced his signature-worst robot anyone has ever seen.

Shelby offered to give me a ride. There is a cold breeze, but I have my aunt's bike. I've been using the two-mile trek as part of my work out routine. I pass through the faculty parking lot and cut the corner at the auditorium. Twenty feet from the bike rack, I notice something's not right. My aunt's bike is on its side with the front basket stomped flat into the wet grass. The handlebars are twisted completely around. The seat is gone.

I curse out loud and try to lift the bike, but the wheels are bent.

My first and only thought is Gooch. I take a step back and look around. People are still leaving the school. Cars are stacked at the parking lot exit.

Two other bikes are chained to the rack. Both are upright

and untouched. I picture Gooch going berserk on the bike because who else would do this? Who else thinks that nothing can touch him? Who else believes there are no consequences?

I swallow a mouthful of anger, kick at the dirt and look back at the school. It's not going to be fun telling my aunt. She warned me to be careful with her bike. "It may not look like much, but I've had it a long time and it's a good solid ride," she'd said.

My phone buzzes with a text. I open a photo of my mother and Jerry, standing under a blue sky in front of a fountain.

- *Just got to Vegas! It's a dry heat! LOL! miss ya!*

I type: *i just won a big match*

Then, I delete it. What's the use of telling her anything? She never listens to me.

The wind kicks up. I raise my hoodie. At the edge of the woods, leaves spiral to the ground. I consider calling my aunt and check the time. Two-thirty. She's working and won't be able to talk.

I shoot a text to Shelby.

- *u still here?*

My phone buzzes:

Shelby: *w my dad what's up?*

Principal Hoffman strides across the parking lot in a hooded parka and buckskin work boots. Shelby walks fast, keeping up. She's in her usual sweats and tights.

They stare at the bike, faces blank, eyes without depth.

"You rode it here this morning?" asks the principal.

"Yes, he rode it here," answers Shelby. "How else would it get here?"

The principal doesn't respond, doesn't even turn to her. He grabs the bike's frame, tugs and holds it upright. "Unlock it," he says.

I squat and flip the numbers on the lock.

The principal lifts the bike away from the rack.

"Is that the seat?" He points to it in the high grass near the woods. "Get it and let's put it all into the car." "Can we check the cameras with you?" asks Shelby.

He hoists the bike to his shoulder, hangs it across his back and starts walking.

"Dad, wait, this is a crime scene," she says. "Shouldn't you leave it for the police? Suppose there are fingerprints or something."

The principal doesn't turn around.

Shelby and I look at each other.

We catch up to him at the back of his Durango. He pops the hatch and slides the bike in. I place the seat next to the bike.

"Mike, get in. I'll take you home," he says evenly.

"Wait a minute," says Shelby. "What about the cameras? Aren't you going to check them?"

The principal goes to the driver's side door and opens it. "That's for me to worry about."

"We should do it now," she says.

He impatiently gazes at the sky then back at her. "That's not happening."

"Why?"

"Did I ask you to get involved?"

"Really?" she says sarcastically. "You're kidding me. Dad, I'm already involved. I'm a witness."

My phone buzzes. My mother again.

Someone has taken a photo of her standing next to a woman sandwiched between two large boards painted like a playing card.

Mom - *met the queen of hearts LOL*

"Dad, I don't think you should have moved the bike," argues Shelby. "You didn't even take a photo. Now all you have are the cameras and what if they weren't working." She turns to me. "Sometimes the security guard forgets to reset the monitors."

Principal Hoffman's jaw muscles grind tight at the sides of his face. I'm sure his next word will shoot a stream of fire. "Both of you, get in the car," he orders.

"Dad, I have my car here," protests Shelby.

"Then Mike," says the principal. "Let's go."

I reach for the car door.

Shelby blocks me with her body. "Mike, say something. Tell him you want to check the cameras? You have every right to know who did it and we both know who it had to be."

Principal Hoffman sighs. "Shelby, how about if just this once you stay out of it."

"Mike, call the police," she demands. "My father can't stop

you from calling them."

"I'd like to keep it in-house," growls the principal. "The school doesn't need the police involved."

"It's because it was Gooch and you know it," says Shelby.

"We'll see," he answers.

She puts her hands on her hips. "And if it was him, what are you going to do about it?"

"He's going to replace Mike's bicycle."

"That's it," exclaims Shelby. "His dad orders one on Amazon. Big deal."

"Right now that's what I'm thinking." His eyes flash at me. "Is that enough for you, Mike?"

For some reason, I feel guilty about all of it. Like I caused all this commotion and trouble. "I'd have to ask my aunt," I mutter.

"I'm sure something can be worked out," he says. "I'm sure we don't need one of our students with an arrest record."

"Then you saw the cameras," says Shelby. "You know Gooch did it. Don't you?"

"I don't know anything except it will be handled properly by me," he says. "And not by you."

"Really?" says Shelby. "Why should we believe anything you say when it comes to Gooch?"

"Could you give me one ounce of respect?" he barks. "Is that too much to ask?"

"Dad, what don't you get about this? Gooch went too far. You can't let him get away with it."

The principal looks exhausted, like he's about to give in. "Come on, Shelby. I've heard enough out of you today."

Shelby gnashes her teeth. "Enough of what? Enough of exactly what?"

"Enough of you and your smart mouth. Now Mike, in the car!"

"No, I'm taking him home." Shelby grabs my hand and tugs me across the parking lot.

I don't exactly agree or disagree with Shelby. I do want to view the camera footage. I don't want to piss the principal off any more than he already is. I look back because I'd rather go with him and settle this man to man. "Come on," says Shelby.

"Your father-."

"He's going to let Gooch get away with this," she says. "I just know it."

She leads me into the school and down the main hall. The overhead lights are off and it's sort of spooky. We pass the teacher's lounge and come face to face with the school's custodian.

"Hey Mr. Tyler," says Shelby. "My dad left something in his office. Could you open the door for me? Please."

The custodian, an old guy with gray hair parted on the side, flashes a smile. "You do know it's Saturday," he says. "You're supposed to be home doing school work." He laughs at his own joke.

"Pretty please," she says in a squeaky voice. "It won't take long."

Still grinning, his eyes track to me. "You're the new buck in town. I saw you put an ass whuppin' on Andrew Fox." He holds out his closed fist.

I pound it.

We follow him to the principal's office. He fingers a wad of keys attached to his belt, separates one and opens the door.

Light slants from a high window where cacti in flowerpots line the sill. The air feels trapped and dead. A neat secretary's desk holds a leather blotter, an old fashioned push-button phone and metal boxes marked IN and Out.

"Okay, go get it," says the custodian.

Shelby crosses her arms over her chest. "Now Mr. Tyler," she says. "It's not going to be that simple. My dad sent me to look for something so I don't know how long it will take."

The custodian lets out a breath and asks, "What are you looking for?"

"My mother's car keys. He grabbed both sets this morning, or thinks he did, and my mother is calling him a scatter brain."

It's a first-rate lie. I'd believe her and give her an Academy Award.

"Ok, five minutes," he says. "If you don't find them in five minutes, I'm throwing you out."

After he goes, Shelby closes the door and locks it. She whispers, "If I told him I wanted to view the cameras, he'd call my father, for sure."

We cross through the principal's office to a small windowless room stacked with monitors, three high, three across. The screens flash black and whites of the school's stairwells, the cafeteria, the gym and the auto shop. On the desk is a laptop. She opens it and powers on.

"Sometimes my father lets me play around with this system," she says. "You can do some serious spying. I once zoomed in on two teachers making out in a stairwell."

"Do I know them?"

Shelby laughs. "Just kidding."

She types a pass code. The screen opens, enlarges. She zooms in on the bike rack and hits reverse. Kids zip backward past the rack. Autumn leaves flutter up from the ground and return to the trees. Principal Hoffman, Shelby and I appear on the monitor. Still in jumpy reverse action, Principal Hoffman takes the bike off his shoulder and lowers it to the rack. I am last to depart from the screen. She hits play. No one passes for about two minutes. Then, a single figure enters the picture. No doubt, it's Gooch. He's got his hoodie up, but there's no mistaking his flared shoulders and the flash of his sharp nose and chin.

"I knew it," says Shelby, pointing at the monitor. "Didn't I tell you?"

Gooch stomps and tramples the bike. He twists the handlebars and flings the seat through the air. His anger is ferocious.

"Man, he really, really hates you," says Shelby.

His meltdown lasts about forty-five seconds, then he looks around and walks off camera.

I think about him in the JV gym, dejected, complaining of a hangover, scared to wrestle Fox. He's not just a coward, he's a punk. A wave of fury rolls over and through me.

"Let's find him," I say.

Shelby screeches around turns, and tells me about a day, two years ago when Gooch threw an orange from the wrestling bus window and nailed a woman in the head. "He never owned up to it," she says. "The team had to stay after practice and run wind sprints for a week and we all saw him do it. The whole time, he acted like the ultimate smugster, like he didn't care, like throwing fruit was legendary or something."

She burns down a local street at fifty miles an hour and hangs a turn sending everything sideways in the car. I keep one hand braced on the dashboard.

"And you still went to the junior prom with him?" I say.

She gives me a quick look. "I know, don't rub it in."

"What if we don't find him?" I ask.

"I know where he hangs out," she says. "We'll find him and let him know he's not getting away with it."

On Main Street, she stabs the brakes. "That's his car," she says excitedly.

His Mustang is head-in at Crusty Grandma's Pizza.

Shelby cuts the wheel, sweeps into a spot and kills the engine. The air in the car feels super charged. I stare at the back of Gooch's Mustang and think of everything I've earned in Molly Pitcher and how fast it can be lost.

"You can't let him get away with this," she says.

My hands are already sweaty. What if I told her to leave and let her father handle it?

"Don't be afraid of him," she says. "He's a complete poser."

"I'm not afraid of him," I say.

"Don't you see?" she says. "Letting Gooch get away with this is what my father wants? He's only worried about what Mr. Goochinov might do. What Mr. Goochinov might say." Her mint green eyes have me pinned in my seat. "For all I care, Mr. Goochinov can take the wrestling dinner and shove it."

I open my door. "Let's go."

We cross the lot between the parked cars. Gooch pushes out of the pizza parlor. He has a pack of cigarettes in his palm and one in his lips. The door opens again and LaRocca steps out. He's devouring a folded slice of pizza.

Shelby walks right up to Gooch and pounds her hands on his chest. "You are such a pathetic coward!"

The cigarette falls from his lips. "What's your problem?" he shouts.

"You're so dumb, that's what *your* problem is."

"Me? I'm dumb?"

"You forgot about the cameras at the school!" She has her face inches from his. "You did, didn't you? You walk past those cameras every day and you completely forgot."

People leaving the pizza parlor stop on the sidewalk. Two little girls holding sodas are wide-eyed.

"We watched the video," shouts Shelby. "You're going to pay for Mike's bike."

Gooch's face bunches up in anger. I get the feeling he's

going to do something crazy, maybe take a swing at Shelby.

I step between them and LaRocca takes my arm. I jam my hand into his face. He drops his pizza and I'm ready for him to come at me, but he doesn't make a move.

Shelby is pointing her finger over my shoulder, calling Gooch a loser. "And you hurt me," she says with her voice disintegrating. "I thought we had something. But, you only wanted one thing from me."

Gooch surges forward. I shove him back and shout, "Back off, Gooch! Back the fuck off!"

He lurches and throws a raking punch. I duck under it. His fist smashes Shelby in her face. The world seems to stop for a moment. Before I can move, she's falling backward off the curb between two parked cars. Her head smacks the asphalt with a thud.

Gooch tries to shove past me. Every cell in my body is screaming, keep him away from her. I grab his sweatshirt. He seizes my head in his hands and digs his thumbs into my eye sockets. "Get out of my way," he shouts.

I throw an uppercut punch and crack him under his jaw. His eyes flutter, then his hands drop. He crashes to the gum-spotted cement like a gunslinger shot in a western.

The crowd around us is a wall of shocked faces.

I pull Shelby to her feet. She keeps saying she's all right, but there is blood clotted in her hair and on the back of her neck. We step up onto the curb where Gooch lies completely still. His eyes stare at the sky and his mouth hangs open.

A half dozen people point phones at us, recording our every

move. My eyes swim over the crowd and stop on LaRocca. He's standing behind the spectators like he doesn't know any of us.

"Nobody go anywhere," says a woman. "I called nine-one-one. The police are on the way."

I hold Shelby tight to my chest. "What happened to Gooch?" she whispers. "Did you hit him?"

Sirens grow louder, close in and pierce the air.

Chapter 28

SEEING MY AUNT come rushing into the police station is almost the worst part. Her coat flaps open, showing her colorful gym clothes. She's so tall and big boned, so out of place next to the uniformed officers and men in suits. I know she doesn't need this trouble and doesn't need me. I tighten my muscles against the hard wooden chair and pull at the handcuff on my wrist. It's attached to a metal ring bolted to a battered desk. I've been in plenty of fights and been caught before, but this has never happened, especially when it was self-defense. It takes all my strength to keep my face from crumpling.

"I'm his guardian," she announces loudly. "He's a minor. Did he tell you he was seventeen?"

The policeman at the front desk lets her pass.

"How is Shelby?" I ask.

My aunt's pretty eyes are glassed with tears. "Right now you have to worry about yourself. We both do."

I ask again about Shelby.

She schusses me, tells me not to say anything. "Not a word, do you hear me," she says. "They use everything against you."

"If you know, tell me," I plead.

"She's at the hospital with the other boy, that's all I've been told." She looks around the room. "I hope you didn't tell the police anything."

When she says this everything I'm feeling gets a little bit worse because I already told them all of it. They know about the bike and about Shelby and me sneaking into the principal's office to watch the cameras. They know I hit Gooch. "Only once," I'd said.

"Did he hit you?" asked a detective.

"No."

"Then why did you hit him?"

"He was trying to blind me."

"And why's that?"

"I was keeping him away from Shelby."

The detective wrote something in her notebook.

"You see," I said. "He swung at me and hit Shelby."

"Why did he swing at you?"

"Because Shelby was yelling at him for wrecking my aunt's bicycle. I got between them."

"And that's exactly how it happened?" asked the detective with disbelief in her voice.

I swore to it and knew that telling the truth in this town, where I have no past, where kids live in McMansions and drive classic Mustangs and two-door Beamers to school, didn't mean anyone would believe me. I knew this, but also knew withholding information would be as good as lying. And, I'm not a liar.

The detective photographed me, tucked my arm under hers, told me to relax my fingers and rolled my prints. She kept saying, "Let me do the work."

Embarrassed, worried, humiliated, I stared at the marred floor and empty jail cells with real bars on the doors. After I washed the ink off my fingers, she handcuffed me to her desk, gave me a bottle of water and a ham sandwich, packaged with one half on top of the other. The bread was stale. I ate it anyway.

"What did you do?" whispers my aunt. "I mean, what exactly did you do."

I'm cold and still I'm sweating. I lift my shirt and dry my eyes. I notice the detective left my phone on her desk. I grab it to text Shelby and see I left Facebook open. On my news feed a shaky fight video plays, already with two hundred and forty seven likes.

Aunt Maggie and I watch Shelby wag her finger in Gooch's face.

I listen to Shelby's words, *You only wanted one thing from me*. At the same time, I remember what Gooch said in the gym, *I've been there and done that.*

I realize this wasn't only about a bicycle or being on the varsity team. Gooch must have hurt her, probably used her. It makes me hate him even more. The video plays on. Gooch's wild swing sends Shelby off the curb. The camera returns back to Gooch gouging my eyes until my fist comes from nowhere, fast as the snap of a whip.

Aunt Maggie gasps, pulls her hand off my shoulder and covers her mouth.

The detective, who took my fingerprints, returns. She's young with soft brown hair and wears her black gun half tucked under a wool sweater. She smiles when she sees my aunt. "Maggie, is Mike your son?" she asks.

Wiping tears, my aunt explains that I'm her nephew, moved up from Florida, finishing high school in Molly Pitcher.

The detective turns to me. "I take her aerobics class," she says. "I'm a devoted follower."

"Did you see the video?" asks Aunt Maggie.

"Yes," she says. "I just watched it with my lieutenant. He's showing the chief." The detective slides in behind her desk. "It appears, at least from the video, that your nephew wasn't the aggressor. But, we do have a problem. A young man's jaw is broken."

A queasiness courses through my stomach. I take a sharp inhale. "What about Shelby? How is she?"

"Two stitches," says the detective.

"That's it?"

The detective sort of smiles. "Head wounds like to bleed. Sometimes they can fool you. The doctors are watching her for a concussion."

Through the squad room window, my eyes land on Mr. Goochinov and Principal Hoffman. For a moment, they stare back through the glass.

"What's going to happen next?" asks Aunt Maggie.

"That depends," says the detective. "This one is a real

Charlie Foxtrot, if you know what I mean."

My aunt and I look at each other, then back at the detective.

"Cluster F-," she says and smiles. "Stay here, I'll be back."

I rattle the handcuff on my wrist. Stay here? Is that cop humor?

"Why didn't you wrestle him to the ground," whispers Aunt Maggie. "Isn't that what you're good at? Why did you have to hit him so hard?" She exhales a soft curse. "And who taught you how to punch like that?"

My phone rings. It's my mother.

"Let's leave her out of it," says my aunt.

I let it ring twice more, then answer.

"Ma?"

"Hi, honey, you'll never guess what I'm doing right now?"

"What?"

"I'm at the chapel with Jerry. We're making arrangements for the wedding tomorrow. The ceremony is going to be sort of tacky, no forget that, it will be tacky, but in a good way."

My head whirls with the information. "Why are you doing this? You don't have to. I can be there for you and the baby."

"Jerry is trying," she says sweetly. "He's going to apologize to you. Believe me. We've discussed it."

"Trying?" I say. "He burnt our house down."

The detective's eyes flick sideways at me.

"Oh, come on now," says my mother. "It was an accident and who isn't growing it?"

It hits me that it has always been this way? Her making

excuses, me thinking next time things will be different.

"Mike, honey, are you there?" she asks.

My aunt takes the phone out of my hand. "Annie," she says sternly. "We are in a police station and your son has been arrested. Yes, another fight. I don't want him saying another word on the phone."

Aunt Maggie listens then says, "No, I'm not joking. He's sitting in front of me wearing a handcuff. Yes, of course he's upset. Annie stop it. I'll handle all of it and get back to you."

She ends the call and puts my phone in her giant pocketbook that's strapped over her shoulder. She closes her eyes, opens them and says, "Talking to her never does any good."

I look at my aunt, so powerful and level headed, so unlike my mother.

The detective returns. She takes her handcuff key out and unhooks my wrist. "Okay, so this is where we're at. For the time being, the Goochinov's are not pressing charges as long as you're not going ahead with any charges."

"What about Gooch?" I say. "He hit Shelby."

"That's going to be up to Shelby and her family," says the detective. "So, you're free to go."

Showered with my stomach full of my aunt's version of a Greek salad, "nothing artificial with nonfat feta and sliced Greek olives," I lie across my bed watching the fight video blow up. Several versions have popped onto my wall. In one, the camera rises to Gooch's angry face, then wheels to Shelby hitting her head. A slow-mo version has a close up of spit splattering from Gooch's lips as my fist crashes under his jaw. Like in the old Batman series, the words "CRUNCH," then "POW," cross the screen. In stop action, Gooch collapses in stages, interposed with scenes of the Hindenburg bursting into flames. When Gooch's knees buckle, the blimp crashes to the earth and a high-pitched announcer begins a rant, "Oh the humanity. And all the passengers screaming...."

The video has 3,732 likes.

I also have seventy friend requests. I recognize a few of the names from my classes at Molly Pitcher and some from Daytona Beach. The rest are unknowns.

Under the video, comments stretch down the screen.

- *I'm like who punches a girl?*

- *Didn't expect that clapback*

- *Gooch had that coming. LMAO*

- *ha ha thts wut i wanted to do to gooch like since the first grade*

- *Is Shelby ok? Is that blood on her head?*

- *I heard that Florida Mike is in JAIL!*

- *Gooch hit a girl = reject*

- *Shelby got stitches she's home*

Adam LaRocca: *not funny - Gooch has broken jaw*

- *too bad for goooch-e-goo*

- *Did he lose any teeth??*

- *Shelby is a DIVA divine*

- *I think she's HOT*

- *u know FL is thirsty 4 Shelby!*

Janice Eng: *Everyone thinks this is so funny? Shelby went to the hospital and Zach has a broken jaw!*

- *Gooch needed to get woke so lighten up*

- *he just did get woke lol*

- *u got that right*

Tara Reston: *Mike - how r u, still causing trouble- ha ha miss ya. I quit that stupid job im @ target doing days way better. When r u coming back call me*

My phone rings.

Shelby says, "I just got home. Where are you?"

"My aunt's. I tried to call you like forty times."

"Oh my God, everyone's saying you're in jail."

"Gooch's father isn't pressing charges, at least not today. He spoke to my aunt and wants to work out a deal. I forget about the bike, he forgets I broke Gooch's jaw. The only problem is, they're forgetting about me. I'm not letting Gooch get away with hitting you."

"Mike, we both know he was aiming at you."

"He swings first and I get arrested. Anyone with eyes and a half a brain can see that he started it."

"Have you gone on Facebook?" she asks.

"Yeah. Nobody has anything better to do?"

"It's on YouTube too," she says. "The fight has like a thousand hits. My parents are on the phone with their lawyer. They want the video taken down."

"It's creeping me out," I say.

"There's a new video where somebody put the president's head on Gooch's body. I almost laughed."

I ask her if she can come over.

"As soon as I got home from the hospital my parents grounded me," she says. "My father is raging. And you'll like this part, when we met you in the parking lot today at the bike racks, he had already seen the cameras. He knew Gooch did it. Now, he's blaming me for the whole thing because I looked at the cameras."

"Aren't your parents pissed off about Gooch punching you?"

She lets out a laugh, "You'd think so, right?"

I sigh. "The way you fell and smacked your head, it makes me sick."

"I'm okay. I've gotten stitches before. The worst part was the nurse shaved a spot on my scalp." After a moment she says, "I wish you hadn't hit him so hard."

"Me too." I pull back the blankets on my bed, slide in and tug them to my chest.

"Gooch is still at the hospital," she says. "They're keeping him overnight. His jaw is fractured and he needs dental work. I don't know exactly what that means. You might have knocked his teeth out."

I shut my eyes and feel my entire being collapse. Will I ever learn from my mistakes? Did I have to hit him that hard? Did I?

"You won't be thrown off the team," she says. "My father is mad at me, not you. He saw the video. He knows Gooch had it coming. Hold on."

I hear the phone drop. "Thank you," she says. "Yeah, I'm talking to Mike."

Then she's back.

"My brother brought me a cup of hot tea with honey," she says. "For once he's not being a dick."

"Is that all you know about Gooch?" I ask.

"Just this," she says. "If I know him, he'll be back to being an asshole real soon. Don't worry."

Chapter 29

I HEAR MY PHONE buzzing on the floor next to the bed.

"Hello."

"Honey, is that you?"

"Mom?"

"That ungrateful ingrate put me out."

I rub my eyes. "Jerry?"

"Yes, Jerry."

"What time is it?"

"Late."

I pull the clock radio over. It's 1:37 in the morning. "Have you been drinking?"

"If you're asking me if I had a few, then yes and paa-leese don't go reminding me about the baby. Not tonight, okay. I know all about having a baby. I had you, didn't I?"

I feel my blood stir and switch on the bedside lamp.

"Where are you?"

"The strip in Vegas. Jerry and I had a terrible fight. The wedding is off. I never really wanted to marry him, not after the way he treated you."

Slightly relieved, I shut my eyes.

"Did you hear me? The wedding is off."

"I heard you. Where's Jerry?"

"I don't know. We were in the casino and he gambled away his money."

"How much?"

"Too much. Mike, if I told you, you'd be sick."

"Tell me."

"Six thousand."

I let the amount sink in. It's more than I thought it would be.

"Now don't go asking me how he earned the money, just don't go there."

I choose my words carefully, "Because he didn't earn it. It's drug money, right?"

My mother is silent.

"You can't even admit it?"

"Stop being a bugger. You didn't even ask me about my ankle."

"How's your ankle?"

"I should write a best seller called, *What Not to Do When You Break Your Ankle.*"

"What does that mean? Is it healing?"

"I guess it's healing, but it hurts all the time. I'm limping and it's throwing everything off."

"What did the doctor say?"

"I didn't tell you?" she says. "Jerry's motorcycle insurance wasn't paid up. So I have absolutely nothing, no coverage, no health insurance."

I can't help myself. "Not a leg to stand on."

"Oh, you think it's funny?"

"Sorry. Bad joke."

"A few minutes ago a man came up to me and gave me a dollar, like I'm some homeless person."

"Really?"

"Yes, really."

From her tone of voice, I know she expects me to supply answers, advice, help her. Tonight, I can only ask, "What are you going to do?"

"Well, yesterday, Jerry, the genius, cut the cast off my ankle. He said removing it would make it easier to get around. You know lighter, but every step was so painful. I taped the thing back on my leg. So it's a mess. I can't get the cast tight enough."

Now, I am fully awake and sitting up in bed. I imagine her under a neon sign, a pool of colors reflected on her face, wearing a dilapidated duct-taped cast.

"How are you doing?" she asks. "Is my sister feeding you?"

I realize she must have forgotten we'd spoken at the police station. I know it's the drinking. "Nothing new here," I say.

"Well, it's supposed to be a surprise, but I know you hate surprises."

"What now?" I ask.

"I've decided to have the baby in New Jersey. I can't do it alone."

"You're coming here?"

"Maggie talked me into it. I can pay for my own plane ticket. I don't need anyone's charity."

There is silence on the line, and then she is crying. In the completely quiet house, I listen to her cough and try to catch her breath. I slide my bare legs from the sheets and stand at the window as her terror and loneliness hits me.

Finally, she heaves a heavy sigh and says, "Maggie is going to find a second-hand crib and a changing table."

"I can help pay for diapers and whatever. I have a job," I say.

She sniffles, "I know and I'm very proud of you."

"Have you gone back to our house?"

"Dotty from across the street called and said it was bulldozed. The bank will take the property. I won't get a cent from them. Jerry dug through the ashes trying to find my jewelry. He smelled like fire for two days. Couldn't get it off his hands."

It hurts to hear this. It was my home. Growing up on that block, knowing all the neighbors, it meant something to me.

She says, "Jerry found a few things."

"What?"

"Most of my jewelry and, believe it or not," she says with some lightness, "one of your trophies was completely untouched. Like it had it's own special power. Mike, I swear to you, it's perfect."

I feel a surge of pure relief. So I didn't lose everything.

"Only that one trophy survived," she says. "I'll bring it with me when I come to Jersey."

I tighten my lips against my braces. "You know what mom," I say almost happily. "You really piss me off sometimes."

"I know."

"When you get here your act is history. Aunt Maggie won't have it. She's not like you. She doesn't associate with people like Jerry. And if you think you're going to have one or two drinks while your pregnant, you can forget that."

"Well good," she says surprising me. "I like to hear you talk like a man. When the baby comes, he's going to need a big brother."

"Do you know if it's a boy or a girl?"

"I did find out there's a fifty percent chance you'll have a little sister." She laughs and coughs.

She is impossible. Completely impossible.

We say goodbye. I return to bed, mash my pillow and lie with my eyes open. What if I could stop being mad at my mother? What if she could actually start over?

"Big brother," I whisper. I'll be eighteen years older than the baby, older than my mother was when she had me.

In the dark, I feel under my bed for my laptop. I take it beneath my blanket and go to Shelby's FB page. I watch her wrestling videos until my eyes are closing. I still notice a bit of hesitation before she takes a shot. I PM her:

Shel, my mom is coming to Jersey to have the baby. Fingers crossed. That's the plan right now. It could be different in the morning. But that's the plan right now.

A minute later, I'm asleep.

Chapter 30

PRACTICE IS OVER and I'm outside the girl's locker room waiting for Shelby. We have been ordered to attend a meeting in Principal Hoffman's conference room. Gooch and his parents will be there. Part of me dreads what's coming. Do I need to hear the principal discuss my school record? The fight with Kyle Scruggs is sure to come up. How do I make them understand that I didn't go to that pizza parlor to break Gooch's jaw?

Shelby pops out of the locker room. Her blown-dried hair is a bouncy mane of curls. She's also put on a lot of mascara and beige eye shadow, which makes me think of Nefertiti in my Egyptian Studies textbook.

She bats her eyes at me. "Do you think it's too much?"

"I don't know," I say, honestly. "Maybe."

She bumps her hip into mine. "Big help."

We stroll the empty hall, leisurely zigzagging one side to the other. Neither one of us wants to go to the meeting. My fingers occasionally touch hers, but we don't hold hands.

"I think this is going to be completely weird," groans Shelby. "I mean, we're supposed to say what we feel with Gooch sitting right in front of us."

"My aunt says it's going to be like that game show, *Let's Make a Deal*."

"Never saw it," says Shelby.

"My mom used to have it on when I got home from school," I say. "It's the show where the contestants dress up in costumes and try to choose the door with the best prize. So like door number one might have a can of beans behind it, door number three, an old pair of boots and then door number two has a washing machine."

Shelby steps in front of me like she's stopping traffic. "We don't need to make a deal. We didn't do anything wrong."

"Maybe we did," I say. "If we had listened to your father and let him handle it then-."

"Don't even go there," she says. "My father should have been honest with us. Why didn't he tell us he knew it was Gooch? Why protect him? Why keep it a secret?"

I shrug and think of the other reason she and I had tracked Gooch down to the pizza parlor. Gooch had hurt and used her, maybe ended their friendship, or a lot more.

When we arrive at the conference room, Aunt Maggie pushes up from her chair at a long polished table. "Here they are," she says.

Principal Hoffman, Coach Rankin, Mr. Goochinov and a woman, who must be Gooch's mom, turn their heads. Gooch is facing the opposite direction and doesn't turn around.

"Come in, come in," says the principal. He stands, absolutely tall and solid looking in his suit and tie.

I step past him and get my first look at Gooch's face. Breath leaves my lungs like I've been slammed on the mat. A stiff-looking metal wire emerges from a patch of bloodstained surgical tape on his cheek and snakes around his face to his front teeth. Somehow the wire attaches to a mass of clips and more wire. What scares me most are his eyes. They hold nothing. It's like everything in him has been removed and replaced with darkness. In front of him on the table are a pen and a yellow-lined pad. It takes me a moment to realize that he isn't able to speak.

My stomach twists and my mind goes to Kyle Scruggs' uneven gaze. I screwed his eyes up forever and now here I am again.

Across from Gooch's parents and Gooch, Shelby and I slip into black and chrome swivel chairs. Nothing feels right. Eyes dart at me. I wonder if this meeting is an ambush. Are the police going to arrive and take me away? Maybe they should.

Under the table, a warm hand encloses mine. My aunt.

"For those of you who haven't met my wife," says Mr. Goochinov, "this is Victoria."

Gooch's mom squints at me like she's noticed a disgusting bug, then half smiles at Shelby. "I hope we can put this behind us," she says. "We've missed you around the house."

"I don't think things will ever be like they were," says Shelby, bringing her eyes to Gooch.

A tall bald man in a leather bomber jacket and stone washed jeans arrives. I've seen him at Mr. Goochinov's side and know he's Adam LaRocca's father. He shakes hands with Gooch's father and places his briefcase on the table.

"I've asked Walter LaRocca to oversee this meeting as my legal adviser and counsel," says Mr. Goochinov.

Shelby huffs out a breath and says, "No way, not him."

Everyone looks at her.

"I mean, didn't anybody ever hear of that expression, like father, like son?"

"Now, what's that supposed to mean?" asks Mr. LaRocca.

Shelby stares at her dad, waiting for him to say something.

He clears his throat. "She's right, let's handle this between the families." He looks at Coach Rankin. "And, Coach, you can stay, of course."

Mr. LaRocca's eyebrows shoot up. "If it's because of what Adam said," he stammers.

"Yeah, it is," spits Shelby. "Maybe you should go back to where *your* people came from."

"That's uncalled for," says Mr. Goochinov. "I invited him here as my attorney."

"Shelby is right," says Aunt Maggie. "I didn't bring an attorney and no one told me you were bringing one."

"Walter, I think you should go," says the principal.

"Yeah, that's a good idea," says Shelby.

Mr. LaRocca opens his briefcase and slides papers across the table to Mr. Goochinov. "Then I'll go."

Everyone watches him leave.

Shelby gets up and slams the door. "Good," she says.

The principal points his finger at her. "You sit down and be polite," he says. "Or, you'll wait in the hall."

"With my own people?" she says and makes wide eyes at her father.

Coach Rankin clears his throat, "Before we do anything, I'd like to put something on the record?" he says.

"What record?" asks Aunt Maggie. "Is this being taped?"

Mr. Goochinov swells his cheeks and lets out a long breath as if Aunt Maggie is trying his patience. "No one is taping anything," he says. "And Coach, if you have something to say, will you do us all a favor and just say it?"

The coach takes a folded paper from his inside jacket pocket, opens it and pushes his glasses up his nose. "I'd like to read a quote from Lord Chesterfield."

"Who the heck is Lord Chesterfield?" whispers Gooch's mother.

"Google it later," quips Mr. Goochinov. "Right now it doesn't matter."

The coach begins to read, "*Young men are as apt to think themselves wise enough, as drunken men are to think themselves sober enough. They look upon spirit to be a much better thing than experience, which they call coldness. They are but half mistaken, for though spirit without experience is dangerous, experience without spirit is languid and ineffective.*"

The silence in the room is as loud as a bomb. I'm hoping no one laughs because the coach sounded completely sincere.

"Sort of says it all," adds Coach Rankin. "Don't you think?"

Gooch's mom's eyes travel from her nails to the coach's face and back. She mutters something under her breath.

"Yeah, it does," says Shelby. "S*pirit without experience is* *dangerous*. I get that."

"Let's start at the beginning and try to figure out how we got here and where we'll go from here," says the principal. "I'm giving my daughter two days suspension for breaking into my office and being an instigator. I feel that's fair."

Shelby shrugs it off.

The principal turns to Gooch. "Zach, as you know, you've been given a week's suspension."

Gooch doesn't move a muscle.

"Okay, some facts," says Mr. Goochinov. "My son was at fault. There's no denying it. The school's video doesn't lie. If Zach hadn't vandalized the bicycle, we wouldn't be here right now."

"Not *the* bicycle," says Aunt Maggie. "It was *my* bicycle. The one my parents bought for me when I was fifteen-years-old. The one my nephew rode to school that day."

"We all know that," says Gooch's mom. "My husband didn't mean any disrespect."

"You pick out a bicycle, any one you want, and it's yours," says Mr. Goochinov. "You want one of those new mountain bikes, it doesn't matter. Tell me what you want and I'll get it delivered to your house."

"A new bicycle is fine and appreciated," says Aunt Maggie. "But you can't buy your son's way out of this and wash your hands like nothing happened."

"I'm not excusing his behavior," says Mr. Goochinov. "Zach is very sorry. What he did was impulsive and wrong. He was angry and disappointed with his wrestling season."

"What he did was criminal," says Shelby.

Mr. Goochinov swivels his eyes to me. "But, it still didn't give that boy the liberty to break my son's jaw?"

"I didn't mean to hit him that hard," I say.

"You didn't mean to hit him that hard," repeats Gooch's Mom. "Now that's precious. Because *you* did hit him that hard and from what I've heard this isn't the first time you've hurt your classmates."

I slip a little lower in my chair. Although Gooch swung first and five thousand people saw it on YouTube, I still feel no better and feel little relief. Because didn't I know I was going to hit Gooch when I arrived at the pizza place? From the day I met him, I felt it coming. Why didn't I just dislodge his hands from my face and push him away?

Gooch's mom tells me to look at "her son." I raise my eyes.

"A broken jaw," she says. "Do you think that's fair? I don't. No, I don't think it's fair at all. I haven't slept one full night since it happened." Resentment covers her face bright as her lipstick.

I have to ask it. "What about his teeth? Are they okay?"

"Yes," says Gooch's mom. "That was the only saving grace."

Gooch scribbles something on his pad and holds it up. He's written, *Not aiming for Shelby.*

"And you think that makes it okay?" says Shelby. "So what if you weren't aiming for me. All it proves is that you started it."

"Shelby, enough," says her father.

"No, I have to say this." She turns her eyes to Gooch. "You never gave Mike a chance. You hated the fact that he was better than you, better than anyone on the team. Hated that he knew moves you never heard of. You tried to beat him down when he could have turned our team around, given us what we were missing. We all knew it. Even Coach Rankin knew it."

The coach leans forward. "Mike still has a chance to make a difference for us." He smiles at me.

"But, Zach, your ego, it couldn't let that happen," says Shelby. "Could it?"

Gooch says nothing, writes nothing. His eyes stay glued to the table.

"I know a lot of you think this is all Mike's fault," says Shelby. "Oh, if he hadn't joined the team," she sing songs. "Well, it wasn't his fault." She sets her eyes on Gooch. "You didn't like losing the wrestle-off to me, did you? A girl. It was beneath you. Instead of trying to be a better wrestler, you took it out on Mike."

"That animal didn't have to hit my son like that," blurts Gooch's mom.

"Don't you dare call him an animal," growls Aunt Maggie. "Your son was trying to blind him."

Gooch's mom points a long finger over the table at me. "There was no trouble before that one joined the team. Everyone got along. They knew their places. Even Shelby had a weight class. Doesn't that tell you something?"

"Oh no you don't," exclaims Aunt Maggie. "I'm not going to let you blame my nephew. Did anyone here read what was written about him on Facebook? I saw it and it literally tore my heart to pieces. It was disgraceful and mean."

I take a huge look at my aunt wondering why she didn't tell me she'd seen the posts.

"Zach, you should know," says Shelby bitterly. "I was the one who wanted to find you that day. I wanted to see your face when I reminded you about the school cameras. I kept thinking you couldn't be that dumb, but you were, weren't you?"

Coach Rankin holds up his hands and shouts, "Let's all cool it! We're here to take responsibility and do better. It's a painful thing to look at ourselves honestly and admit our mistakes. I'm sure there isn't anyone in this room that wouldn't do things differently. I know I would. I should have seen this coming. For God's sake, it was a slow moving train."

Gooch raises the pad. In block letters he's printed:

MIKE I AM SORRY

SHELBY I AM SORRY

Tears spurt from his eyes. He lowers the pad to the table, writes furiously, then holds it up:

I should have wrestled Fox. I know that now.

He drops the pen and pad and covers his face. Sobs quake his body.

His mother puts her arm around him. He tries to shake her off. Mascara tears run down her cheeks. "Last year we had a wonderful season," she says. "Absolutely wonderful. This one was supposed to be even better."

Part of me knows what Gooch's mother has said is true. I turned the team upside down. Gooch warned me, but I couldn't leave Shelby alone. I met her in the mornings before school. I encouraged her to wrestle-off Gooch and told her to take back her weight class. Everything Gooch thought was locked down became unhinged. What he knew to be true, wasn't anymore.

Like it's catching, Shelby's eyes fill with tears.

I fight the knot forming in my throat.

Gooch's father gives Zach a handkerchief and says, "Pull yourself together."

I open my mouth to say I'm sorry, but the words don't come. What happened can never be erased. Forever I'll be the wrestler who broke Gooch's jaw. I want to believe Gooch will forgive me and heal, yes eventually heal. My throat loosens. "I'm sorry," I say. "Gooch, I'm really sorry. I shouldn't have hit you like that."

Shelby pushes away from the table. "Can we just say this is over, here and now?" she asks loudly.

Chapter 31

THE PARKING LOT is already full when we arrive at Seaside High School. I get out of the rear seat of Principal Hoffman's Durango. Shelby unbuckles from the front, hooks her backpack over her shoulder and hops out. Looking tough in maroon sweatpants worn low on her hips, a short dungaree jacket and leather gloves with the fingers cut off, she twists her neck to one side then the other and inhales slowly though her nose. I know she is calming her nerves and mentally preparing for the night.

She gives me a nervous smile. "I just was thinking," she says. "All guys worry about losing to a girl. Tonight there are no guys and I've never lost to a girl." She grabs my hand. "So tonight's my chance to learn how it feels."

"No, tonight you will win," I say.

All week we met after practice in the aerobics' room at W-O-W. Shelby brought her laptop and studied the stats of the 132-pound female wrestlers in South Jersey. Ten times a night I told her to stop over thinking the tournament. "Don't you understand," she shot back. "A lot of people want me to suck so they can say, '*You see, I told you she didn't belong on the Minutemen.*'" While we were perfecting an escape, she told me about getting an early acceptance to Douglas College at Rutgers. "It's an all-girl's school," she said. "I don't know if I want that, but the women's wrestling team is one of the best on the East Coast."

I started to say, Go for it, but decided it would be smarter not to. A girl like Shelby will have lots of choices to make and plenty of good advice.

The high school lies prison-like, low and long with a flat roof and tan bricks. Shelby and I follow her father through a side door. Inside, it's like any school anywhere. Same hot-lunch smell, same green lockers, same bright posters announcing, Chess Club, Year Book, Student Council. We join a group of parents and wrestlers and follow handwritten signs that say:

Wrestlers > This Way ☺

The gym buzzes with coaches, parents, wrestlers, brothers and sisters. Women in bright singlets and wrestling shoes are spread across a sea of blue foam mats that form four wrestling rings. Shelby falls into a registration line that's five deep with female wrestlers. Moms and dads at a folding table are collecting twenty dollars from each participant. Wrestlers get a shirt that says, *Tri-County All Girls Tournament* and a chance at the first-place two-foot trophy, the second-place silver medal or the third-place bronze medal. Final finishers in each weight class go on to wrestle the Northern Jersey champs. Eventually, one woman will be awarded the state title in each weight class.

Shelby moves up in the line, shifts from foot to foot, raises one arm, grabs her elbow, and stretches her shoulder. I wait next to the principal, who is shaking hands and being greeted by parents as they pass by. For me, the night feels like a new beginning. I have never been to a woman's wrestling tournament and to make it even more exciting, I am officially dating one of the wrestlers. I gave Shelby a silver bracelet, secretly picked out by Aunt Maggie at the mall. She wore it to school today.

"You hungry?" asks the principal.

I am starving. I haven't eaten since an anemic-looking turkey burger at lunch.

"Come on," says the principal. "Let's get something. My treat."

I follow him through the crowd to the snack table.

More than ever, I need to watch my weight. I'm not sure when it happened, but I've grown from five-ten to five-eleven. Aunt Maggie marked it on her kitchen wall. 138-pounds, which had once been the obvious weight-class for me, is now a battle. I'm dying for a hot dog or one of those baseball-glove sized salted pretzels. I select bottled water, a banana and a zero-fat protein bar.

The principal buys two slices of square pizza, a can of lemon-lime Gatorade and pays for everything. We enter the gym, climb the bleachers and set the food on the bench below.

The protein bar is like eating chocolate covered sawdust. I uncap the water bottle.

"So what's new with you?" asks the principal.

"Nothing much." I watch the action on the mats and remember my aunt's last phone conversation with my mother. They talked about converting a room at the back of my aunt's house into a nursery. My aunt had gone on and on about the coming preparations for the baby. "Yes, Annie, you'll absolutely take your old bedroom back. The crib will fit next to your bed," she said. "And I'm buying a pullout couch for Mike." Happy tears broke in my eyes, yet part of me still doesn't believe she'll ever come to Jersey. She's living at her cousin's condo in Ormond Beach. It's a seasonal rental. She could stay there all winter, which would give Jerry plenty of time to get back in the picture.

"Gooch returns to school on Monday," says the principal. "Luckily, it was a simple fracture. He's eating solid food again."

I still have Gooch in my head. When I least expect it, when I'm watching TV or doing homework, I see him holding up his pad, MIKE I AM SORRY. I haven't figured out a way to make it up to him or his family. Maybe I don't have to, maybe just knowing I'll never hit someone again is enough.

"Your honest opinion," says the principal. "What are Shelby's chances tonight?"

I watch a wrestler jump rope. She's about Shelby's size and weight. Half her head has been freshly shaved to bare brown skin. Her shirt says, *I Break Mine to Kick Yours*. "Chances of winning it all, or taking home a medal?" I ask.

"Winning it all," says the principal.

I would like to say, it doesn't matter. But, it does. For Shelby tonight is about proving she's for real, proving that her varsity letter is not a gimmick or her way of getting attention. One thing I've learned from wrestling is there is always someone better than you. Tonight the top female wrestlers in the county are here to win. Some will start out strong and win their first two brackets. By their third match, their muscles will be fatigued, nerves shot. Running on adrenalin, they are more likely to make mistakes.

"She has the will to win," I say. "That's for sure."

I watch the many women on the mats. Their colorful singlets flash as they execute warm-up moves. I peel the banana and take a bite.

The principal smacks me on the arm. "What about your season? Pretty exciting so far."

I don't like to think about being undefeated. Even talking about it is a jinx. "I want to keep it simple," I say. "Stay at 138 and see what happens. Next year, I'll put on some muscle and go 145."

"You still looking at schools in Florida?"

"My old coach is at Southeastern University," I say. "But I'm probably going to try for Rutgers." Saying this out loud for the first time feels dangerous, like I just kiboshed my chances. My way to Rutgers, or any college, will be on a wrestling scholarship.

Shelby returns dressed for combat. She pulls a red bandana low on her forehead. Her shiny Lycra singlet is bright blue with "USA" across her chest in white letters. The face of a bald eagle rises up her right thigh. Her body is solid, not an ounce of extra weight. She looks balanced, fierce and elegant. She slips on her headgear and buckles her chinstrap.

"What?" she says to me.

"Nothing."

"You were looking at me like something's up."

I want to tell her how good she looks, how the singlet shows off her wide shoulders and the curve of her hips, but that would be completely weird.

She steps into silk shorts and pulls on a t-shirt that says, *You Don't **PLAY** Wrestling*.

"Come on," she says. "Warm me up."

I don't have any gear with me. I take my house key and phone out of my pockets and ask the principal to hold them. Shelby and I find an open spot on the mat. She stares straight across at me; five seven in her flat-soled wrestling shoes, exactly a hundred and thirty-one and a half pounds. "Let's start with the ten basic moves," she says.

I take a shot and miss.

"So, that's all you've got," she says playfully.

We lock up. She executes a driving double and lifts me off the mat. I fall with her. In the scramble, she earns the takedown and locks her legs around mine.

We face off again. She shoots, takes my leg and tumbles me to the mat. Her speed is amazing.

"Now get a move in your head," I say.

Her eyes light, "What makes you think I don't have one?" She seizes my wrist. "You want me to tell it to you?"

I try to roll away from her, but she's pulling me in.

"Ball and chain," she grunts.

"Then do it." As the words leave my mouth, my arm is yanked between my legs and she's cranking me over onto my back. I fight the move, but there is no escaping. Shelby has me tight, locked down.

Her father shouts, "Shelby, nicely done!"

She releases me and smiles proudly.

I sit on the mat admiring her. My heart swells with the sight of her bright smile. Today she will wrestle Jersey's best women. I will be at the side of the mat with her father.

Shelby and I set up again. Her eyes shine like emeralds. We lock up and I wait for her next move.

About the Author

T. Glen Coughlin was born in New York City and grew up in Freeport, NY. He received a BA from Hofstra University and an MFA from Columbia University. His first novel, *The Hero of New York*, W.W. Norton, was completed when was 23 years old. It explored the dark side of the middle class suburban dream. His second novel, *Steady Eddie*, Soho Press, is a coming of age story set in Long Island. In 2012, Harper Collins published his first YA novel, *One Shot Away, A Wrestling Story*. It has received critical acclaim.

I Lost To A Girl is his fourth novel.

Acknowledgements

Special thanks and recognition goes to Mike Faccone, the wrestler who inspired this story. Also, the author wishes to thank his son, Thomas, his daughter, Jacqueline, his sisters, Kathy Banicki, Laura Quinn and Susan Grempel, early readers, Georgene Shanahan and Lauren del Cid, fellow writers, Lyn Stevens, Mary Sternbach, Kevin Singer, Tim Tomlinson and Richard Price, wrestling coach and educator, Chris McGrath, and editor, Juris Jurjevics, who sadly passed before this publication. And always, and especially, love and thanks to his wife, Laura Ellen, for her patience and perseverance.

Without these people, there would be no book. He thanks them with all his heart.

Made in the USA
Middletown, DE
24 February 2021